D0430955

RICHMOND TALES

LOST SECRETS OF THE IRON TRIANGLE

RICHMOND TALES

LOST SECRETS OF THE IRON TRIANGLE

Summer Brenner

Illustrations by Miguel Perez

 Time & Again Press

Cover design and book design by Jan Camp.
Cover and interior illustrations by Miguel Perez.

Citation: *Three Little Fishies,* words & music by Saxie Dowell, 1939.
Photographs are courtesy of the Richmond Museum of History Collection.

ISBN:0-9779741-4-6

www.timeandagainpress.com

Please note: This narrative contains offensive words that
have been used because they reflect the attitudes and
parlance of particular historical periods.

For more information contact:
Community Works West
1605 Bonita Avenue
Berkeley, CA 94709
(T) 510-845-3332 • (F) 510-649-8239
community_works@yahoo.com • www.communityworkswest.org

The writing, design, and first printing of this book was underwritten by a generous grant from the Creative Work Fund.

In addition to the Creative Work Fund, I would like to acknowledge the inspiration and help of Don Bastin; Chic Dabby; Steve Gilford; Coco Liboiron; Lincoln Elementary School in the Iron Triangle and its principal Mimi Melodia and teacher Eric Verprauskus' fifth-grade class; and the spirit of John Malloy and William Morris. My thanks also go out to Malcolm Margolin; Linda Norton at the Regional Oral History Office (Bancroft Library, University of California, Berkeley); Lyn Palme at Contra Costa Library; the Richmond Library archives; the Richmond Museum of History; Megan Shaw Prelinger and Rick Prelinger and the Prelinger Library; Betty Soskin; Michael Weber; Jane White; and the World War II Home Front National Historic Park and Archives.

A special word of appreciation to Ruth Morgan and Community Works; Rodney Ferguson at Richmond's Literacy for Every Adult Project (L.E.A.P.); Marin Trujillo and the West Contra Costa Unified School District; West County READS; and above all, my children, Felix Brenner and Joanna Bean.

Table of Contents

PART I • RICHMOND NOW

PART II • RICHMOND THEN

PART III • THEN, NOW, AND LATER

This book is dedicated to the youth
of Richmond, California—
and to youth everywhere who do not yet know:
there is a there there.

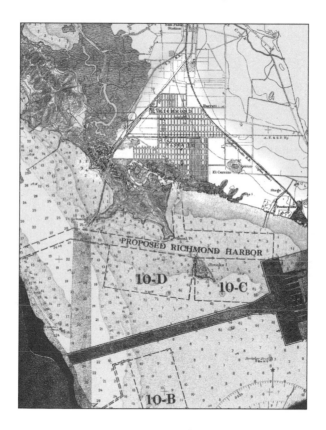

PART I

RICHMOND NOW

Welcome to the Iron Triangle

Maisha Yates walked along Macdonald Avenue, gazing above her at the trees that lined the street. She walked, listening to the crunchy sound the leaves made beneath her feet. She stooped down to pick up a few dry leaves and stuck them in the pocket of her hoodie.

She wished there were a forest nearby so she could run through it. She wished there were a safe place to sit and think. "Someday, I'll go to a real forest," she muttered, closing her eyes and trying to imagine the cool silence, the leafy canopy of trees, and the mixture of pungent smells.

Macdonald Avenue was the main thoroughfare in the Iron Triangle, an old section of Richmond, California. Maisha went to school in the Iron Triangle. She was born in the Iron Triangle. Her two best friends, Yasmine and Carolina, were born in the Iron Triangle, too.

Usually, they walked together. However, today Maisha had gotten in trouble. Today, she had to stay after school.

As she shuffled along, she glanced at a boarded-up house. Its big yard had plenty of towering trees, chattering birds, and busy squirrels. However, Maisha was not allowed to go into the yard.

"Under any circumstances," her mother warned her.

Empty lots and abandoned houses were off-limits to most kids in the Iron Triangle. They were dangerous. Sometimes, drug dealers congregated there. Sometimes, homeless men used the premises to camp out or drink. Sometimes, gangs drove by and shot at the windows. Maisha did not need a warning. She went out of her way to avoid these places.

As she approached her apartment house, she walked more slowly. Once home, she would have to tell her mother what happened in school. She would have to show her the teacher's note.

"What question did you ask out of turn today?" her mother, Linda Yates, demanded.

"I asked why we call our section of town the Iron Triangle."

In exasperation, Linda Yates put her hands on her hips and glared at Maisha. "You've already asked that question. I don't know the answer, and your daddy doesn't know the answer. Did your teacher know?"

Maisha shook her head. She had even asked her friends, Carolina and Yasmine. They thought Maisha asked too many questions.

No one seemed to know the answer. The next time her school library was open, she planned to ask the librarian. As for the public library, the closest one was twenty blocks from her house. She was too young to walk so far alone.

Whenever Maisha asked her mother to let her take the bus to the library, Linda reminded her that it cost almost a dollar to go and almost another dollar to come back. Her mother usually didn't have two extra dollars.

"Why can't you sit in class and listen?" Mrs. Yates reprimanded Maisha.

The girl stood beside the kitchen counter, chewing her thumb.

"You can't find your tongue now, but at school, you wag it all day long, don't you?" her mother accused.

"I guess I'm curious," Maisha admitted.

"No 'guess' about it," her mother's voice rose angrily. "What am I supposed to do with you? Your daddy has gone to get work in Texas. I'm here in Richmond, working as hard as can be. It seems to me, Maisha Yates, you can do your share. Your job is to go to school, get good grades, and not upset your teacher. You hear me?"

"I hear you," Maisha said, blinking back her tears.

Not only did Maisha hear, but everyone on Barrett Avenue heard, too. Her mother might as well announce to the whole world that Maisha Yates was in trouble.

The Cooper Brothers

Linda Yates worked at UPS in Richmond. Maisha was proud of her mother's job. She liked that her mother wore a uniform and drove a truck. What she didn't like was that the hard work wore her mother out. On weekends, Linda Yates was usually too tired to go off and do anything fun.

"Honey, I'm sorry about today," Linda said wearily. "Next weekend, I promise."

Maisha exhaled a sigh of disappointment. Since her father left to work in Texas, she and her mother almost never left the Iron Triangle.

"Can I ask a friend over?" Maisha asked although she already knew the answer.

"It's not a good day for company," her mother predictably said. "Why don't you check on our flowers?"

Maisha stood at the window that overlooked the back of their apartment building. In between the patches of brown grass, the only bright spot was a bed of flowers. Last spring, she and her mother planted pale yellow snapdragons, foxgloves to attract hummingbirds, sweet-smelling rosebushes, and a border of bright blue lobelia.

Although the flowerbed was beautiful, weeding and watering were not what Maisha had in mind for Saturday afternoon.

In addition, there were unwelcome newcomers to the neighborhood who usually occupied the patch of grass and the nearby bench.

Early in September, Sammy and Shannon Cooper moved in with their grandmother in the apartment house next door. The Cooper brothers acted as if they owned the ground, the grass, the bench, and the world. They told Maisha she couldn't sit on the bench unless she asked permission.

"Are those Cooper boys outside today?" Linda Yates wondered aloud.

They were outside almost everyday because they usually cut school.

"If you ignore them," her mother advised, "they will leave you alone."

Maisha had tried to ignore them. She had tried to make herself invisible as soon as she walked outside.

"Hey, freak!" Shannon shouted if he saw her. "You didn't ask permission to walk on my sidewalk."

If Maisha pretended not to hear, they asked, "Are you deaf or what?"

Her mother said the boys were trying to intimidate her.

"Intimy-what?" Maisha asked.

"To feel tough, they have to pick on someone smaller and younger." Linda Yates put her arms around Maisha and gave her a big hug. "It's sad for you, but it's also sad for them. The Cooper brothers are lost out in the world. I feel sorry for them, too."

"I don't!" Maisha cried.

"A nice boy moved into our building last week. While I take a nap, why don't you go introduce yourself to him?"

Maisha's face puckered in a frown. "Like knock on a boy's door who doesn't speak English and say what? I don't think so."

The truth was Maisha no longer had Latino friends. Now that she was older, it had become hard for kids from different backgrounds to kick it. In kindergarten, Maisha's best friend had been Mexican. In first grade, her best friend came from Laos.

9

Somehow, things had changed. Black girls hung together. Latina girls hung together. Asian kids had their own clique. The few white girls hung out with one of the other groups. Boys were separate. So was everyone who didn't look like her.

"Have you even said 'hello' to him?" Linda asked.

"I'm not supposed to talk to strangers," Maisha reminded her mother.

"He is not a stranger. He's a new neighbor. Their family just moved to Richmond. The least you can do is make him feel welcome."

"I have to write a report," Maisha frowned again.

Looking out the window, she could see the intimidating Cooper brothers and their friends. They were sprawled on the bench, smoking and laughing.

Before Maisha ducked, they looked up. "Hey, freak!" They yelled and slapped each other five.

Maisha clenched her fists. She wished the earth would open and swallow them whole.

Banging Down the Door

"I'm sorry, did I scare you?" A boy stepped out of the shadows. "I dropped the mail key. Now, I can't find it."

"Whatever," Maisha commented, sifting through a stack of magazines on the floor of the entry hall.

"If I scared you, I'm sorry."

"Whatever," she said again, inspecting his messy hair and ugly shoes.

"I just moved in," Mario stuttered, trying to restart the introduction.

"I know," Maisha replied in a tone that suggested she knew everything.

"My mother asked me to invite you up to our apartment," he stammered.

Maisha shook her head. "My mother wouldn't approve. She doesn't allow me to talk to strangers or visit their apartments."

"But," the boy blushed, "my mother had a conversation with your mother. I don't think she would mind."

Maisha was surprised at how well the boy spoke English. He spoke as if he had been born in Richmond, too.

"My name is Mario," he said.

"I'm Maisha," she replied coldly.

"Mario and Maisha? They're almost the same," he commented.

"Whatever," Maisha said, trying to ignore him.

Desperately, Mario tried to think of something clever to say. It was obvious that he was not making a favorable impression.

"Hey, freak!" a voice yelled from outside the door. "Open up for a visit!"

The menacing words were followed by loud knocks that shook the glass portion of the front door. Another voice laughed and also banged on the glass.

"The little freak found herself another freak," Shannon Cooper roared. "Now open the door!"

Mario looked at Maisha. Her eyes were wide with panic. The magazines shook in her hand.

"Do not open under any circumstances," she whispered urgently.

"Hey, retard, you want to live until dinner?"

12

"I just moved in," Mario stuttered, trying
to restart the introduction.

Four boys pressed their faces to the glass of the door. They banged away, laughing and yelling threats.

Mario grabbed Maisha. He pulled her under the stairs where they crouched behind the smelly garbage bins.

"Who are they?" he whispered.

Maisha gasped for breath. She felt sick to her stomach, partly from fear and partly from the smell of soiled diapers and rotten food.

"Do they live here?" Mario asked.

"Two live with their granny in the next building," she said as the wave of nausea passed. "I don't know the others."

The raucous banging continued for a few more minutes. However, the boys failed to break the door. The glass was protected by thick wire mesh. Finally, they got bored with their game and went away.

Maisha sighed with relief. Mario sighed, too.

Recently, Mario and his family had moved from Los Angeles to Richmond. He had not wanted to move. In Los Angeles, he lived in a Mexican neighborhood. He had good friends. He had his *amigos* who protected him.

"What do they want?" he asked.

"Whatever," Maisha said, trying to sound cool again.

"Are they high?" Mario wondered.

Maisha had seen people on drugs, but they didn't act like those boys.

"Maybe, they're crazy," Mario concluded.

Maisha had seen crazy people, too. They didn't act like those boys.

"Maybe, they want to steal everyone," Mario said.

"*Steal*?" Maisha giggled. "You mean, *rob*."

"Yes, rob everyone."

Maisha said nothing. She had lived in Richmond all her life. She had seen drunk people and drugged people. She had seen people fight. She had seen a boy shot. She had seen her auntie go crazy. These were terrible memories that she wished would go away.

However, no one had ever tried to make her life miserable until Sammy and Shannon Cooper moved into the neighborhood.

"They're trying to intimidate us," she finally said.

Mario looked at Maisha, eye to eye. Although he was unfamiliar with the word, he understood her meaning.

"I don't know what 'in-timmy-date' means," Mario admitted. "But I don't like it."

Hopes and Dreams

The weather in Richmond had turned cold. The air was chilly and damp. Streets and sidewalks were filled with leaves. Soon, the last blooms of Linda Yates' flowers would wither and die. Soon, the winter rains would come to Richmond.

Mario's mother, Sylvia Reyes, cleaned houses for wealthy families in Berkeley and Albany. Unlike Linda Yates' work schedule, hers was flexible. Her work did not exhaust her. She had free time on the weekends.

The following Saturday, she invited Maisha to come to the library and the movies with her and Mario. This was a big treat for Maisha. Nobody had extra money for the movies, and her friends never wanted to go to the library.

Maisha had big hopes and big dreams. She wanted to go to college. Her best friend, Carolina, wanted to go to college, but Carolina never tried hard at school.

Yasmine, her other best friend, said, "Girls from Richmond don't go to college. Girls from Richmond either drop out of school, or get pregnant, or work at Wendy's."

Maisha knew what Yasmine said wasn't true. Nevertheless, part of her feared it was true. Part of her feared one of those things could happen to her.

With Maisha and Mario buckled in the back seat, Sylvia Reyes drove their station wagon along Macdonald Avenue. They puttered past Eighth Street, Ninth Street, Tenth Street, and the city's lush garden at the corner of Harbour Way.

"Pretty garden," Mario said, surveying the flowers and trees and colorful murals of birds, butterflies, creatures, and kids.

"It's my favorite place in Richmond," Maisha confessed.

"Mine, too," Mario smiled. "I want to study plants when I go to college."

"I'm going to college," Maisha said confidently. It felt good to say the words aloud.

"I want to be a doctor," Mario said.

"A doctor?" Maisha was intrigued.

At school, boys bragged about their future fortunes with the NBA, the NFL, and the Major Leagues. No one ever said that they wanted to be a doctor.

"Don't you have to go to school forever to be a doctor?" she asked.

"I made up my mind after my cousin died," Mario said gravely.

"Just like that, you decided?" Maisha snapped her fingers.

Mario's voice choked with emotion. "If I had known what to do, I might have saved him."

Only recently, Maisha had vetoed any friendship with Mario Reyes. However, things had changed. She had discovered she could say things to Mario that Carolina and Yasmine would never understand.

As the station wagon dipped under the railroad overpass, the Amtrak and BART trains whizzed out of the station.

Maisha had traveled twice on BART. Once, she went with her daddy to watch the Oakland A's play the Yankees. The second time, her parents took her to the Ringling Brothers' circus at the Coliseum.

Maisha had never crossed the Golden Gate Bridge nor visited San Francisco, but her two BART trips gave her a keen taste for traveling. She hoped that when she grew up, she would travel the world.

Mario never boasted, but in fact, he was a real traveler. Every year, he traveled by plane to Mexico. Once in a while, he even traveled southward from the California border by train for over forty hours.

"If it takes so long, how do you sleep?" Maisha asked.

"We sleep in our seats," Mario explained.

"And eat?" she wanted to know.

"We bring baskets and boxes of food with us. It's a big picnic because everyone on the train is Mexican. Everyone is going home to see their families. Everyone is happy."

"Do you have a passport?" Maisha probed.

"I have two passports," Mario blushed, knowing he had finally impressed Maisha.

Macdonald Avenue dipped and rose on the other side of the BART station. On the eastern side, Richmond felt like a different city. The atmosphere was more open and less dangerous. The houses and yards were prettier than the west side where Mario and Maisha lived. There were fewer drug dealers and fewer gunshots. After dark, the streets didn't have the ghost-town feeling of the Iron Triangle.

"Hey!" Mario pointed.

Leaning against a fence at the corner of Twenty-third Street and Macdonald were Sammy and Shannon Cooper.

"Did they see us?" Maisha asked anxiously, dropping her head below the car window.

"No," Mario sighed.

Like Maisha, he wished the earth would open and sweep them away.

Bad for the Heart

On Sundays, Maisha often visited her great-grandmother in North Richmond. North Richmond was on the northern end of the Iron Triangle. However, it was not part of the city of Richmond. It was isolated from the city. It was its own separate place.

Some parts of North Richmond felt almost rural. Other parts were filled with boarded-up buildings, vacant lots, industrial yards, and warehouses. Surrounding many of the buildings were rusty, corrugated fences, topped by rolls of razor wire.

Recently, a few blocks of Third Street had been rebuilt. Attractive flowerbeds and benches had been added to a median that divided the street. A health clinic, senior center, and new housing had been constructed, too.

Although North Richmond was not far in miles, it took a long time to get there by bus. Maisha did not mind the bus ride. It was long and boring, but at least, it was safe.

What made Maisha nervous was the walk from the #74 stop on Market Street across Rumrill to Verde Avenue.

Some of the way, she and her mother had to walk on the asphalt road because chunks of sidewalk were missing. Men on the street corners called out to her mother. They tried to talk to Maisha, too. Sometimes, they offered them drugs or asked them for money.

"First, acknowledge them," Linda Yates advised. "Then, look straight ahead and keep walking. Don't get into their business. Don't let them get into yours."

"How come you're not afraid?" Maisha asked.

"I am afraid," Linda admitted. "But a long time ago, I found out that it's bad for the heart to live in fear."

"You mean this heart?" Maisha pointed to her chest.

"Yes, it's bad for the muscle inside your body," her mother explained. "It's also bad for your other heart, the one that puts goodness into the world."

Maisha thought about her second heart. Sometimes, hers was open, but often, it was closed. Sometimes, her heart tried to do good. Other times, it was filled with mean and ugly thoughts.

Linda Yates added, "You have to develop antenna so you know which dangers are real. If we're afraid, we can't change. We get stuck, afraid to move forward and afraid to take chances."

Maisha was glad that Linda was her mother. She was glad that her mother gave her good advice. Some of her friends were not so fortunate.

Yasmine's mother was unstable so Yasmine lived with her aunt. Carolina's mother had asthma and diabetes. It was hard for Carolina's mother to breathe.

Neither Yasmine nor Carolina knew their fathers. They both looked up to Maisha's parents. They talked about Linda and Simon Yates as if they were their parents, too. They liked to ask Maisha when daddy Simon was coming back from Texas.

"How do you get antenna?" Maisha asked uncertainly.

Linda Yates threw her head back and laughed. "Sometimes, mistakes are the only way. I earned my antenna from lots of mistakes."

At the corner of Truman Street, a group of teens stood in a circle. Rap blasted from a portable radio. A couple of girls practiced dance steps in the street. In the center of a circle, there was a boy. He was throwing a knife at the boards of an old door.

Ping! The knife reverberated each time the blade struck wood.

Ping! The knife danced on the tip of its metal point.

Ping! Each time the knife stuck, the other kids shouted words of praise.

"Sammy is chill!"

"Sammy is bad!"

"Sammy is the bomb!"

Maisha glanced at the boy with the knife. Chill, bad, boss, bomb, it was Sammy Cooper! Beside him was his brother, Shannon. They were her tormentors.

Maisha buried her head under her mother's arm. She didn't want to see them. Most of all, she didn't want them to see her.

"Let's hurry," she whispered.

Suddenly, Sammy stepped out of the circle.

"Hello, Mrs. Yates," he said with a drawl. "Remember me?"

Cruisin' for a Bruisin'

The open knife lay balanced on the palm of Sammy Cooper's hand.

"Of course, I remember you," Linda Yates said calmly. "We haven't seen you in the neighborhood lately."

"They arrested me," Sammy said with swagger. "Didn't you hear about that?"

Sammy tried to make his voice sound tough, but it was still boyish.

"Your granny told me you and Shannon worried her to death," Linda Yates replied. "It's your loss that you can't live with her."

Sammy drew his arm back and aimed the knife at a nearby fence.

"They tried to pop me for 'boosting,' but I beat it," he crowed.

"Looks to me like you're *cruisin' for a bruisin',*" Linda Yates said sternly. "That's an expression we used back in the day."

"Hear that, homies?" Sammy repeated, *"Cruisin' for a bruisin'!"*

Linda Yates looked fiercely into Sammy's troubled eyes. "You might like the poetry," she said, "but I guarantee you won't like the California Youth Authority."

Sammy retrieved the knife. He aimed again at the fence.

"Most ladies don't like knives," he challenged Mrs. Yates.

"Most human beings don't like weapons. Period!" she snapped. "A knife is useful. A knife can cut an apple or slice bread. That's a good thing. But weapons, Sammy, are a curse on everyone. I hope you don't have to learn the hard way."

Sammy smiled. He liked Mrs. Yates. He liked that she always said "hello" and spoke directly to him.

"Is that what you think, too?" Sammy asked Maisha.

The girl shuddered.

Sammy's brother, Shannon, yelled in Maisha's face. "What exactly *do* you think?"

Maisha jumped. That was exactly the reaction Shannon wanted.

Linda Yates stepped up. "Boys," she called them out, "we are neighbors. We live in the same community in the same city. I know your grandmother. I knew your Uncle Eddie before he died. I went to school with your mother. I know your people. I am certain you both can do better than this."

Several teens whistled as if Mrs. Yates had scored big. They waited to see what the brothers would do. There was tension in the air, tension so thick that everyone could feel it. Maisha felt it most of all. She looked around for a car or another adult or a telephone to call for help.

Sammy looked around, too. He was already in trouble. He was in trouble at school and with the law. His grandmother had kicked them out. He and Shannon were on the verge of being separated and going into foster care.

Sammy pushed Shannon aside. He closed the knife. He threw it down on the ground. He held his hand out to shake Mrs. Yates' hand.

"Peace," he said, holding up his fingers in a V.

"Peace," Linda Yates smiled.

Maisha said nothing. She could not understand why her mother bothered to talk to boys like Sammy and Shannon Cooper.

"Maybe we'll see you on our way back," Mrs. Yates offered.

Linda and Maisha continued to walk by the side of the

road. A few cars sped past. Large, noisy trucks lumbered along.

"See," Mrs. Yates said. "He's not so bad."

Suddenly, a loud noise erupted behind them. It was not the high, explosive sound of gunshot or firecrackers, but a big, dull thud.

"Do not turn around," Linda Yates ordered.

However, Maisha had already looked back. Behind her, she spied the windshield of a parked car shattered into dozens of fine, spidery lines. Beyond the car, Sammy, Shannon, and their friends were blurs, racing in the opposite direction.

Visiting Auntie Yates

As Linda and Maisha approached Auntie Yates' house, they saw her seated on her rocking chair. Whether sunny or cool, rainy or hot, Auntie Yates sat everyday on her rocker in the late afternoon, watching and recording the world of North Richmond.

"Hey, girlfriends," she waved at Linda and Maisha.

Maisha opened the gate and leapt up the steps to hug her great-grandmother. "Auntie Yates," she cried. She was relieved to have reached a safe haven. Auntie Yates always made her feel safe and secure.

"I heard the pop and got worried," she said, patting the top of Maisha's braided hair. "It didn't sound like a gun, but you never know around here. It certainly scared Buster."

Buster, Auntie Yates' old hound dog, lifted his long, tired head from his paws.

"Didn't it scare you, Buster?" Auntie Yates asked him.

By way of reply, Buster barked.

"Did you hear it?" she asked Maisha.

"Yes, ma'am," Maisha said.

"Kids down the block smashed a car window," Linda explained.

"More trouble," Auntie Yates said, shaking her head.

In the distance, the siren of a sheriff's car grew louder and closer.

"They don't have anything better to do," Linda sighed.

Maisha blurted out, "They don't want to do anything but cause trouble for everybody else."

Auntie Yates stroked Maisha's hot, angry face. "They scare you, don't they?"

Maisha bit her lip so she wouldn't cry.

"Of course, they scare her," Linda answered. "They're out there crashing and smashing. Who wouldn't be scared? They destroy the little bit of peace we find for ourselves."

"They need something to occupy them," Auntie Yates said. "They have enough energy to change the world, but most have lost hope. They just live day to day. The hope is there, but it's buried deep inside them."

Maisha recalled Yasmine's comment on their future. *College isn't for girls like us. Girls like us either drop out of school, or get pregnant, or work at Wendy's.* Maisha wondered if Yasmine had lost hope, too.

The sheriff's car raced down the street.

"Come in the house while I get cleaned up," Auntie Yates said, wiping her palms on the front of her overalls. Despite the chilly nights, Auntie Yates' vegetable garden still thrived. A few luscious tomatoes clung to their vines; and a dozen slender zucchinis could be found tucked under their leaves on the ground.

Linda and Maisha followed Auntie Yates into the blue parlor. Everything from the curtains to the rugs was blue. The different shades of blue made the room feel like a pond or piece of sky. Auntie Yates said that blue was a healing color. Blue was her favorite color. She said that blue kept her deceased husband, Tommy Lee Yates, close at hand.

Auntie Yates also had another name. People called her "Keeper." Neighbors said Keeper never wasted a rubber band or a piece of string.

Auntie Yates explained, "During the Great Depression when I was raised up, folks really had nothing. In those lean years, nothing was for real. It wasn't as if you only had three pairs of shoes. You had no shoes. Your house was plastered with newspaper to keep out the wind and cold. You had little to eat and almost nothing to wear. If you lived on a farm, the crops were sorry. If you tried to sell what you raised, there was no one to buy them. If you lived in town, there were no jobs."

Linda added, "My people went through those hard times, too."

"Times are still hard, but now it seems people don't help each other the way they used to," Auntie Yates lamented.

Auntie Yates was not only Keeper of things. More importantly, she was Keeper of stories. She kept the stories of the Yates, Prescott, Lightheart, and Lyle families. She also kept other people's family stories. Auntie Yates was the Keeper for the entire community.

Occasionally, a stranger would stop by her house and ask, "Did you know my Uncle Fred? He lived in North Richmond in 1948."

Another stranger would drop in, "I'm trying to find my cousin, Mona. They said she came through here in 1983."

Auntie Yates knew who came and went, who was born and who had died. That's the real reason they called her Keeper.

After Sunday supper, Auntie Yates led Maisha into the bedroom. "I want you to look at yourself," she said, turning Maisha towards the large mirror that hung over the cherry wood chiffonier.

"Your face is changing. Look at the copper-red color in your cheeks that comes from our Cherokee blood. Look at your fine brown skin that comes from our African blood. Look at the streaks of green in your eyes that comes from our Spanish blood."

Auntie Yates stooped so their faces, one old and the other young, were side by side.

"Remember, Maisha Yates, we are survivor people. We had to survive back then. We have to survive here and now, too."

"Remember, Maisha Yates, we are survivor people."

Lines in Air, Earth, Water, and Fire

"Don't bother Auntie Yates with your foolishness," Linda chided.

"Why foolish?" Auntie Yates asked.

Linda Yates exhaled loudly. "Every time Maisha asks this question, she gets into trouble. The principal called me for the second time this month. Maisha's teacher has arranged a special parent conference."

"You don't have time to make trouble," Auntie Yates admonished her great-granddaughter.

"It isn't on purpose," Maisha defended herself. "It's because I'm curious."

"Maisha always was curious. A curious child is a blessing."

Linda Yates sneered, "Her teacher doesn't think that it's a blessing."

"I only keep asking because nobody knows," Maisha explained.

"Keeper probably knows," Linda said. "You'll finally get an answer to your pesky, little question."

"What is it, Maisha?" Auntie Yates asked.

"Why do we call our neighborhood the Iron Triangle?"

Auntie Yates crossed her arms and tilted her silvery head.

"I used to know," she tapped her temple. "But something has slipped out of Keeper's brain."

"The one thing I want to know and you've forgotten!" Maisha cried.

Auntie Yates' eyes brightened. "I know who knows. They call me Keeper, and they call him Seeker."

Linda Yates interrupted. "Please, do not be introducing our Maisha to that man."

"What's wrong with him?" Maisha asked.

Auntie Yates reassured her, "Nothing is wrong with him. Seeker can answer this question and many, many more."

"Is 'Seeker' his real name?" Maisha wondered aloud.

"His name is Misty Horn," Auntie Yates said.

"Misty Horn," Maisha murmured.

"He's a nut, if you ask me," Linda Yates commented.

Auntie Yates cackled. "I admit that he's eccentric. He tells stories of mankind's ways: past, present, and future. He says the past is like palm-reading. He believes you can glimpse the future in the past."

Maisha gazed at the lines on the inside of her palm.

"Misty Horn reads the lines in air, water, earth, and fire. He says if you know how to read these lines, all time is visible."

"All time visible?" Maisha mused.

"He lives in the Triangle," Auntie Yates said.

"That's right," Linda Yates mocked scornfully. "I see him. He's out there doing his thing. He's walking around with his imaginary friends. He's waving his fingers in the air, talking to the present, past, and future."

"Don't be sarcastic." Auntie Yates replied, half-laughing at Linda's description. "A person's mind is a beautiful thing."

"Yes," Linda Yates countered, "but there's also such a thing as *out* of your mind."

Watching Raindrops

"Hey!" Mario shouted.

"Don't shout," Maisha said.

Mario grinned from ear to ear. "But I have new news."

"Not *new* news," Maisha corrected. "News is always new so you don't have to say it twice."

"What's wrong with you?" Mario asked. "You sound upset."

Maisha kicked her foot against the wall. "Not really," she fibbed.

"You look upset," Mario persisted.

Maisha and Mario stood at the front door of their apartment building. Outside, a hard December rain drummed the sidewalks. Leaves from the oak trees filled the gullies on Barrett Avenue. Wind whipped an empty plastic bag across the empty yard.

Mario used to love the rain. The smell of rain recalled

his summers in Mexico. Now, there was a troubling aspect to the rain. Whenever it rained, it was hard for his papá, Manuel, to work. Construction sites usually closed down in the rain.

When Manuel Reyes was working, he was lots of fun. He loved to laugh and wrestle with Mario. However, when it rained, all Manuel did was mope around the house and worry about money. He wasn't fun at all.

"So what's your *new* news?" Maisha asked.

"My great-grandmother is coming to visit. You'll get to meet her."

Maisha indulged Mario with a smile. She knew how much he loved his *abuelita*. He loved her the way that she loved Auntie Yates, but she got to see her great-grandmother almost every week.

"We usually visit her in Michoacan," Mario said. "This year, there's no money to go."

"Michoacan?" The melodic syllables rolled off Maisha's lips. "Is that the same as Mexico?"

"It's a state in Mexico, a beautiful state. It was once a rich kingdom. The name comes from the Náhuatl language: *michin* (fish), *hua* (own) and *can* (place)."

"Too bad we can't visit her," Maisha sighed with discontent.

"Maybe someday, we'll go there," Mario offered.

"I doubt it," Maisha said. "I never go anywhere."

Mario knew that Maisha was sad because her father had to stay in Texas for the holidays. Maisha had never spent a Christmas without him.

"Want to come upstairs and watch a movie?" Mario asked.

"No, thanks," Maisha said. She didn't want to spend another Saturday afternoon in an apartment. She wanted to do something new and exciting, somewhere faraway.

"On second thought, Tio Lito and Papá are probably fighting."

As soon as the words were out of Mario's mouth, a small, wiry man appeared on the stairs.

"*Adiós*," he shouted to Mario, hurrying past.

"Later, Tio Lito," Mario replied.

"I doubt you see me again in your whole life," he yelled as he leapt out the front door.

"That must have been a really bad argument," Maisha said.

"That's Tio Lito," Mario explained. "He's my favorite uncle, but Mama says he never stops by unless he wants something."

"Probably money," Maisha guessed. "My Uncle Lucky is exactly the same."

Lucky was her mother's brother, but he wasn't lucky. Uncle Lucky had a gambling problem. If he had money, he went to the racetrack and lost it. Linda said he should have been named "Unlucky."

Mario sighed deeply. "Papá will be upset all afternoon. He was already upset because of the rain. Now, it will be worse."

"Let's see who can watch the rain without blinking," Maisha suggested.

Maisha and Mario blew on the glass portion of the door. They watched their breath cloud the glass. They stared at the rain. Mario lost the contest because he blinked first.

Outside, cars crawled slowly up and down Barrett Avenue. Occasionally, a siren, en route to Kaiser-Permanente's emergency room, burst through the sound of rain.

The only pedestrian was an old man, walking slowly and holding a carved cane in his right hand. With his left hand, he made signs through the raindrops and in the air.

Maisha and Mario fixed their eyes on the man's freely moving, mesmerizing hand. His fingers noodled the air as if he were playing the piano.

"He's always out there, doing something weird," Mario said.

"I met him," Maisha confessed.

"And you didn't tell me?"

"In case you haven't noticed," Maisha said, "I don't tell you everything. He's a friend of Auntie Yates. She told me they call him Seeker, but his real name is Misty Horn."

"That's cool," Mario commented, staring at the heavy, gray day.

"He asked me to visit him," Maisha whispered secretively. "He said he has treasures to show me, but I don't believe him."

"Let's go," Mario reached for the doorknob.

"Mama won't let me visit strangers."

"But you said you met him," Mario insisted. "You said he's a friend of your *abuelita*'s."

"Mama doesn't like him," Maisha admitted.

"Do you like him?"

Maisha shrugged her shoulders. "He's just a harmless, old man."

From the doorway, they could see Misty Horn's pleasantly wrinkled face: his wispy white goatee and bushy white eyebrows, his totally bald head, and his polished skin that was not quite brown or black or tan.

"He's mixed like my family," Maisha said. "African, Spanish, Indian, and a dash of French. Like Auntie Yates, he's from Louisiana, too."

"He's there," Mario pointed to the short figure at the corner. "He sees us. He's waving. He's asking us to come outside."

806,000 Hours

Maisha and Mario ran into the rain, holding a newspaper over their heads.

When they reached Misty Horn, he turned his cane upside down, pushed a small lever on its stem, and a giant black umbrella opened.

"Cool!" Maisha exclaimed.

"Very cool," Misty Horn agreed. "It couldn't be cooler, even if I hadn't invented it."

"You?" Mario asked in disbelief.

"Someone had to invent it so why not me?" When Misty Horn laughed, his gold teeth glistened, and his bluish-brown, round eyes laughed, too.

"Standing in the rain, it is impossible to imagine I invented anything. All you see is a senior citizen. This senior citizen, however, has lived over 806,000 hours on earth. I've had the opportunity to invent many things."

Maisha and Mario looked at each other with astonishment. Obviously, Misty Horn was unusual, but they were not sure if that was a good or bad thing.

He continued, "My last wish on earth is to reach one million hours. I'm afraid that's unlikely with my ticker. Now Keeper, she'll make it to a million. She'll probably live past one hundred and ten years."

"I hope so," Maisha gulped.

"Don't fret about Keeper. She's as strong as a yak." Misty Horn assured her.

"Yak?" Maisha and Mario uttered at the same time.

"Of course, you won't find yaks around here unless you happen to see one in a zoo. They are wild, shaggy, hairy oxen that live in the mountains of central Asia. Yak milk, yak butter, yak meat, they're very tasty."

"You've eaten yak?" they asked simultaneously.

"Yakburger, hold the mustard and walk it through the garden! In restaurant lingo, that means to load up the lettuce and tomato."

Mario and Maisha smiled. Misty Horn was more unusual than they imagined.

"Sadly, we don't have a yak to pull a cart over to my house on Bissell Avenue. I guess we'll have to ambulate on our own legs," Misty Horn declared.

"We can't go to your house," Maisha announced.

"Too bad," Misty Horn sighed.

"It's raining," Mario explained.

"That's all the more reason to pay a visit to a friend. It's traditional to go visiting on rainy days. Tell me, what else do you plan to do? Homework? TV? Watch raindrops?"

"That's what we were doing," Maisha admitted.

"Yes, I saw you. Watching raindrops is a peaceful activity. It doesn't harm anyone. It lets your mind wander. It's a fine thing, but now I'm here. My house is only a few blocks that way."

Misty Horn yanked the lapels of his jacket up around his neck. He adjusted his pants. He waved his hand in circles, following the mysterious lines of water and air.

Maisha and Mario gave each other a long, deep, puzzled look.

"Run in and tell your folks that you'll return in a little while. Tell them not to worry. Tell them you have to help a senior citizen home."

Five, Six, and Seven Senses

"Come in," Misty Horn gestured as he unlocked the front door.

Instead of forward, Maisha stepped back. She wasn't sure if visiting Misty Horn was a good idea. Mario, however, boldly crossed the threshold.

"Welcome to my humble abode," Misty Horn announced, bending his torso forward in a bow.

"I like those paintings," Mario said, glancing around at the walls, the shelves of books, the array of musical instruments, and the framed sepia photographs. In one of the paintings, he recognized the corner of Third Street and the building that was now the Rescue Mission.

"I painted them sixty years ago," Misty Horn confessed. "I'm what you call a 'Jack of all trades.' I have tried my hand at painting, piano, poetry, piccolo, ping pong, physics, impersonation, philately, photography, and philosophy. All the Ps I could think of."

Maisha leaned through the door. "Impersonation doesn't start with P," she corrected.

"Quite right," Misty Horn waved at her with his magical, mystical hand. "Now come into the house and close the portal to the outside. I'll get a fire going and make hot chocolate. There's nothing like hot chocolate to make us thankful for the rain and cold."

"Painting, piano, ping pong, impersonation which doesn't count, and photography," Maisha enumerated.

"Plus physics, philosophy, and poetry," Mario added.

Misty Horn picked a short, slender silver instrument off the shelf. He blew into one end and held his fingers over a couple of its holes. A sweet, high-pitched song emerged.

"Piccolo," he said. "And that's philately." He pointed to several large, leather-bound albums.

"Is philately like photography?" Mario asked, surveying the albums.

"It's a fancy word for stamp-collecting," Misty Horn replied.

"Why do people collect stamps?" Maisha wondered aloud.

"Why do people do anything?" he snapped in return.

Maisha mulled over the question. She wanted to do so many things that it was hard to decide what to put first.

"Aren't you curious about stamps?" Misty Horn asked impatiently.

Maisha wanted to shout out that she was always curious. She wanted to confess that curiosity got her in trouble almost everyday.

However, Maisha's tongue was tied. She didn't say anything. Suddenly, she was sorry that she ever agreed to visit a grouchy, grumpy old man.

Mario turned the musty-smelling pages of the stamp albums. Each page was heavy black paper. Each stamp was carefully glued on a page and labeled with a date and country of origin.

"I never really looked at stamps," he admitted.

"Now you'll see them differently," Misty Horn said.

From the kitchen, the smell of warm, thickening milk and sweet chocolate filled the house. Misty Horn stirred the pot with a flat wooden spoon. He carried a wicker tray with three bowls of steamy chocolate into the living room.

"Miss Maisha," he offered.

"No, thank you," she replied sullenly. The discussion about curiosity had put her in a bad mood.

"Hot chocolate for you?" Misty Horn turned to Mario.

"Yes, but I never drank it from a bowl."

"It's nice in a bowl," Misty Horn said. "The French drink coffee and hot chocolate in bowls. They lift the bowl and sip it like soup. It's more fun. It lasts longer. Best of all, there's far more room. Wouldn't you say so, Maisha?"

"Whatever," Maisha sulked.

Misty Horn set the tray on a bench by the old-fashioned velveteen sofa. Then, he crouched beside the fireplace, placing twigs and paper on the wrought-iron grate.

"We'll have a roaring fire in no time," he said. "Want to help me, Maisha?"

Once Maisha fell into a bad mood, it was hard to fall out. "I wouldn't know how," she said.

This time, Misty Horn felt the force of Maisha's mood. Perhaps, he thought, he was to blame. Perhaps, it was his tone of voice. Perhaps, his house smelled like he never bathed.

Now, he chose his words more carefully. "Maisha, I want to thank you for paying me a visit today. I only invite special people to my house."

"What makes you think I'm special?" she blurted out.

"I've studied human nature, the greatest of all investigations. I have a seventh sense about such things," Misty Horn said solemnly.

"I thought there were only five senses," Mario said, counting them off. "Taste, sight, smell, touch, and?"

"Hearing," Maisha chimed in. "It's the reason you have two flaps on the side of your head."

"That's right," Misty Horn said. "Now take your bowl of hot chocolate, Maisha. It will conquer all cares. If I've said or done anything offensive, please try to forgive me."

Misty Horn's apology was well-received. Maisha took a seat on the velveteen sofa. She sipped the steamy, delicious liquid.

"Most of us are blessed with five senses," Misty Horn said. "Occasionally, we meet someone with a sixth sense. Take Auntie Yates, the Keeper, she's a walking sixth sense. She knows what's coming and going because of her sixth sense. Some people call it 'intuition.' I bet Maisha inherited a big dose of intuition from Auntie Yates."

Maisha smiled at Misty Horn. He was right. She had excellent instincts about people.

"My *abuelita*, too," Mario said. "Everyone calls her Guardian. She takes care of the rivers and creeks."

"But what's the seventh sense?" Maisha was unable to contain her curiosity.

"The seventh sense is difficult to explain with language," Misty Horn said, waving all his fingers at the same time. "It's about the invisible lines in air, water, earth, and fire."

Maisha rolled her eyes. Maybe, her mother was right. Maybe, Misty Horn was a little cracked.

Three Treasures

"Mexican chocolate is the best!" Mario boasted. "It's the drink of the Aztec kings."

"Indeed!" Misty Horn heartily agreed. "Chocolate was served to the Spanish when they came to Montezuma's palace. In Europe, there was no chocolate or tomatoes or potatoes. Five hundred years ago, Europe was missing many of the delicious things we eat today."

"No french fries!" Maisha cried.

"No pizza!" Mario moaned.

"When you finish your drinks, we'll take the grand tour," Misty Horn suggested.

Mario looked around the small Richmond house. It was plain on the outside with bars on the windows and doors. How much of a tour could there be? he wondered.

"Why do they call you Seeker?" Maisha asked.

"Because I seek the elements of the past, present, and

future with my breath," he winked. "I go around and blow wherever I am. That's how the world gets written down."

Neither Mario nor Maisha understood. Most of what Misty Horn said was too mysterious. He spoke in an esoteric language that only he could fathom.

"Before the grand tour, let's inspect my three treasures," he announced, clapping his hands.

"Treasures?" Mario stammered. The house looked too shabby to contain real treasures.

From a small wooden chest, the old man lifted out a velvet sack. Its corners had been bunched together and tied with a silk cord. Carefully, he undid the cord. Carefully, he unfolded each corner.

Maisha and Mario crowded behind him, conjuring gold nuggets, precious coins, and sparkling jewels. However, as the cloth unfolded, they saw only a rock, a dry leaf, and a mummified seahorse.

Maisha double-blinked with disappointment. Mario double-blinked in return.

Misty Horn said, "These objects contain a vast amount of knowledge, but you would hardly notice them on the street or sidewalk."

"I'd notice the seahorse," Mario piped.

"Me, too," Maisha said, reaching out to touch the parchment-colored skeleton.

"This ordinary rock represents the mineral kingdom, the foundation of our planet Earth. The leaf is a reminder of the treasures of the vast plant kingdom. The little seahorse is the miracle of the animal kingdom." Misty Horn tossed them in his palm like dice. "Here, I carry a twenty-four volume encyclopedia in my hand."

Strange Eggs

The grand tour of Misty Horn's house did not take long. It required exiting the kitchen door, unlocking a metal door, passing under an exterior archway, and climbing a set of steps to a second-story room.

"That's Richmond," he pointed to a large map leaning against the door. "It's one of the first maps made after the railroads arrived."

Included among the grid of streets was a basic, familiar shape. Three sets of railroad tracks formed a triangle. The tracks of the Southern Pacific and the Atchison, Topeka, and Santa Fe formed each side.

"It's the Iron Triangle!" Maisha shouted excitedly.

"Correct!" Misty Horn winked. "You have an excellent eye."

"I've asked everybody what Iron Triangle means. Auntie Yates said you would know."

"Well, it's Maisha Yates who figured it out."

Maisha was pleased. She had solved the answer to her riddle. Now, she could report back to her parents, her teacher, the principal, and Auntie Yates.

Misty Horn pointed to the steam-covered glass of a large picture window on the western wall. "From that window, you can see forever."

"Forever?" Mario challenged. He could see almost nothing. The sky hung like draperies over the house and streets. Everything was shrouded in mist and rain.

Misty Horn elaborated, "Well, I think we can agree that 'forever' is a big concept. It goes *in* as well as *out*."

"But where do you go if you go *in*? Where do you go if you go *out*?" Mario wondered.

"Isn't it clear?" Misty Horn asked.

"Not to us," Maisha said.

"If you travel out, you find the world of space and infinity. If you travel in, you find your own universe. It's your choice."

"Really?" Maisha was doubtful.

"Only if you want to," Misty Horn reassured her. "No one will make you."

Maisha and Mario gave each other a puzzled, penetrating look. Their look said the afternoon was growing even stranger.

"Can you explain the difference between going *out* and going *in*?" Mario asked.

"That's just it," Misty Horn said. "There isn't much difference. It's a question of perspective. When you travel into space or ride in an airplane, you are going out, not up. Coming down, you're actually traveling in. I am a founding member of the *OUT, NOT UP, SOCIETY*. In elevators, I like to re-label the UP and DOWN buttons with IN and OUT."

Maisha's neck was hot, and her hands were sweaty. So far, she had understood nothing of Misty Horn's metaphysics. Nevertheless, intuition told her that she was soon going to understand a lot.

She glanced at Mario. He was sweating, too. Beads of perspiration were strung along his worried forehead.

"Do you think I could have a glass of water?" he asked.

"We'll take care of that in a few seconds," Misty Horn said. "But first, come take a look at these."

Beneath the window, where Misty Horn declared that he could see forever, was a long shelf. On it sat a dozen giant eggs. Each one was a foot long and a foot in diameter.

"Ostrich eggs?" Mario asked.

For Maisha, they looked like the eggs that her cousin, Louise, brought over on Easter. Those eggs were made of hard, spun sugar. One end of the eggs was sliced off and replaced with a clear, little peekaboo window. If Maisha looked through the window, she could see a miniature panorama of sugar bunnies, sugar trees and birds, sugar flowers, and sugar squirrels.

Maisha bent down to look at one of Misty Horn's giant eggs. Like the sugary Easter eggs, it too had a little peekaboo window. Inside was a miniature picture of a marsh, a bay, and fountain-shaped spouts she recognized as whales. There were scores of whale blows in the air. There were seals, lounging on rocks. There was a bear, clutching a large fish. Maisha couldn't tell what the creatures were made of, but it certainly did not look like sugar.

Along the inside of the egg were horizons dotted with green hills and tall trees. At first, it looked like a picture. Then, something stirred in the colors, shapes, and lines as if the picture were really alive.

"I can't see much," Maisha said nervously.

"So you prefer life-size?" Misty Horn asked.

"I like the big picture," Mario looked up from another one of the eggs. In it was a similar coastline. Instead of sea mammals, however, there were docks, cranes, and sheets of metal that fit together to make enormous ships. Thousands of people were going into construction areas, carrying lunch pails and toolboxes. He could not hear them, but he could see that they were laughing and shouting.

"Shall we start at the beginning?" Misty Horn inquired.

"It might be easier to understand," Maisha said.

Misty Horn agreed. "Time, however, is a trickster. It likes to trick us into thinking we always move forward. Perhaps, we are totally still. Perhaps, it is something else that moves."

Neither Mario nor Maisha understood Misty Horn's words, but they sensed his meaning.

"Normally, with a newspaper or television, we can see the world at the same time in different places," Misty Horn observed. "These eggs are exactly the opposite. They show one place at different times. Maisha has been looking at a view of primordial Richmond."

"Richmond?" Maisha cried out. "That's not Richmond!"

"You're absolutely right," Misty Horn agreed. "It wasn't called Richmond. It's not the Richmond you know. However, I assure you that it's exactly the same spot where we are standing now."

Maisha and Mario stared intently into the egg. The picture had slightly shifted. There were two bears, holding a fish in each paw. A herd of elk moved slowly across a vivid green hill. Something had startled the birds. The whole sky was black with their wings.

"Let's start," Misty Horn rubbed his hands together. "Are we ready?"

"For what?" Mario asked skeptically.

"Didn't you say that you're thirsty?" The old man laughed gleefully. "I know where to find the purest water on earth."

*Then, something stirred in the colors, shapes, and
lines as if the picture were really alive.*

PART II

RICHMOND THEN

The Visit

Maisha and Mario concentrated on the egg. The picture had shifted again. The birds, elk, antelope, seals, and whale spouts were still there, but they could also see humans.

However, they did not resemble the sort of humans that Maisha and Mario knew. They were half-naked with strong, muscular figures. They were clothed in skirts made of feathers and animals skins. All of them were barefoot. Their hair was combed and coiffed in strange and unfamiliar ways.

"Let's look inside the next egg," Maisha proposed.

"I'm afraid the water's not so pure," Misty Horn noted sadly.

The old man bent down, pressing his face to the little window.

"Come on," he urged Maisha and Mario, taking their hands. "The more we look, the more we see. The harder we stare, the quicker we get there."

He repeated several times:

The harder we stare,
The quicker we get there.
The harder we stare,
The quicker we get there.

Maisha and Mario tried to resist, but Misty Horn's enthusiastic spirit swept them along. At his urging, they stared and stared. Eventually, they could not keep their eyes open. A strong wind forced them shut. The wind blew around them, encircling them and tossing their clothes to and fro.

When the wind stopped, they found themselves in the center of a meadow. Tall grasses, taller than Maisha and Mario, were everywhere.

"I think the creek is this way, if I remember correctly," Misty Horn said. "However, it doesn't matter. We'll find a creek, no matter which way we walk."

Maisha was frozen with fear. "Where are we?" she gasped.

"We're in Richmond, your hometown," Misty Horn chuckled. "If I had to say exactly, I think we're fairly close to Crescent Park."

"My cousins live in Crescent Park," Maisha said indignantly. "They don't have grass like this. There are buildings and lawns. There are streets and cars. It's nothing like this."

"Come along," Misty Horn said, "before young Mario expires from thirst."

Surrounding them were the sounds of birds, singing, cawing, crowing, and cooing. It wasn't a few birds like the ones that Maisha sometimes heard in the Iron Triangle. It sounded like millions of birds.

"Where are those birds?" she asked, looking around.

"They're in the grasses and trees, by the creeks, in the marshes, and down by the rocky shore. This is their home. They've got plenty of places to nest and plenty of food to eat."

"I don't see anything but tall grass. I don't see marshes or trees or shore."

"Just wait," Misty Horn said. "You'll soon see all of it."

In the middle of the waving green and yellow grasses, they found a well-worn path. The path was almost a foot deep, incised in the meadow by much use. As they stepped onto the path, Misty Horn said, "That's much better. Now, we'll be able to find our way."

"Really?" Mario asked doubtfully.

"The path goes everywhere we need to go," Misty Horn assured him.

"I hope we get to the creek soon," Mario added. His throat was painfully parched and dry.

As the path descended, the grasses sprouted shorter. There were fields of purple, yellow, and red flowers. There were marshlands and a giant bay. In the distance, across the water were land masses, small and large hills, Mount Tamalpais, and a few scattered islands. There were no buildings, no highways, no boats, and no bridges. It was a pristine place.

"I hear the creek," Mario said.

"How come you know it's a creek?" Maisha asked.

"It sounds like a creek, doesn't it?"

"I don't know," she admitted. She had never heard a creek.

"Sure, it's a creek," Mario said confidently. "There's a creek near my *abuelita*'s house in Michoacan. If it's not too dirty, I swim in it. *Abuelita* is guardian of the creek. She keeps out the trash."

"No pollution or trash here," Misty Horn remarked. "You can drink and swim and never get sick."

The path soon led them to a beautiful, rushing creek. The water rippled over glistening rocks, past creek banks, shaded by willows. Large ferns sprouted beside the water. A stand of majestic pines, broad oak trees, and huge redwoods grew nearby.

Maisha shrieked. "I'm not going over there!"

"Shush!" Misty Horn warned. "You'll scare the antelopes."

"What about scaring me?" she cried, staring at a family of large, four-legged creatures.

"They won't hurt you," Mario assured her. "They're getting a drink, too."

"I don't care what they're doing. I'm going back over there."

Maisha reversed direction and skipped back to the oak grove. Although the trees, meadows, and creek were beautiful and filled with lovely smells, Maisha felt out of place. The Richmond that she knew was so different.

In contrast, Mario seemed at home. He was comfortable in wild places. In Mexico, he often went out into the fields to help his uncles herd cattle. He often rode horses and donkeys.

Mario strolled to the creek. He touched the soft rump of an antelope fawn. The baby animal did not budge, nor did the antelope doe. Unperturbed, they continued to drink from the shady creek.

Mario squatted at the edge of the water. He cupped his hand and took a long, cool drink. Being near animals calmed him. At his *abuelita*'s house, he always volunteered to feed the horses, chickens, cows, and pigs.

As Maisha reached the oak grove, another family of antelopes strolled casually past her. "Ekk!" she cried, running back to the creek.

Guardians and Keepers

"Animals feel your fear," Mario said, trying to comfort Maisha.

"I can't help it," she defended. "They're so big."

"Don't let size intimidate you," he said. "They're big, but they won't hurt you."

"Nor do they want to eat you," Misty Horn laughed. "They're peaceful vegetarians. Sometimes an Ohlone may kill one, but all the creatures share the land."

"Ah-low-nee?" Maisha repeated.

Misty Horn grinned, "An Ohlone is a human animal like you and me."

"Really like us?" Mario asked.

"The Ohlone is human but different. They speak, but unless you know their language, you won't understand. They eat, but it's food you probably never tasted. They dress, but you've never seen such clothing. They sing, but you don't know the songs."

Maisha recalled the faraway places she visited in books. Traveling in her own imagination was under her control. Here, in this strange version of Richmond, she felt totally out of control.

"How long do we have to stay?" she wondered aloud.

"I love it here," Mario responded. "I love the smells. I love the peacefulness. I could stay a long time."

Maisha looked at Mario with admiration. He was perfectly at ease.

"Don't you like Richmond?" Misty Horn asked in a teasing tone.

"I don't know," Maisha admitted truthfully. "It's so different."

Misty Horn sympathized. "Differences frighten us, but usually there's nothing to fear."

Maisha flashed back to her mother's words: *it's bad for the heart to live in fear.*

"I've never been any place like this," Maisha said. "Except for squirrels and birds, I've never seen a wild animal. I've never visited a zoo."

Misty Horn patted her shoulder. He said, "Imagine if an Ohlone girl visited your Richmond. Imagine how terrified she would be of trucks and cars. The noise and speed of the eighteen-wheelers would scare her to death.

Instead of marshes, she would see asphalt. Instead of hill-sides, she would see concrete and buildings. If you offered her ice-cream, she would refuse."

"Poor girl," Mario laughed.

"We won't stay long," Misty Horn said. "I just wanted you to experience a world that has vanished. The earth itself is buried beneath the cities. The native Califor-nia trees and grasses have almost disappeared or been overtaken by imported species. The fantastic numbers of creatures—millions of birds, fishes, and animals—are nearly gone."

"What about the people?" Mario asked anxiously.

"A few Ohlone are still around. Some live near Rich-mond. They look like other Americans. Fortunately, a few keep the knowledge of their old language. They sing their ancient songs. They keep their culture from disap-pearing."

"They have Keepers," Maisha said thoughtfully.

"And Guardians," Mario added.

"Seekers, too," Misty Horn said.

"Can we see the Ohlones?" Maisha was growing more and more curious.

Misty Horn's hand twirled around as if he were read-ing the lines in the air.

"Forty small villages are scattered around San Francisco and San Pablo bays, on the coast down to Big Sur, and east in the hills. The villages have different names. The people call themselves by different names and speak slightly different languages. Altogether, we call them the 'Ohlone People.' They have lived here over a thousand years."

Maisha's heart beat faster. Her curiosity overwhelmed her fear. "Can we see them now?"

Misty Horn turned in all directions. "Some men are out hunting deer," he said. "Some women are in the meadowlands, gathering berries and seeds. Other men are in their fishing boats, made of tule rushes. Let's go to the village and see who's there."

Misty Horn turned to follow the well-worn path. Maisha and Mario turned and followed, too.

Dream Friends

Coming towards them was a young girl. She wore an abalone shell necklace that covered her chest, and a buckskin skirt that reached from her waist to her knees. She was barefoot.

Maisha and Mario stared in amazement.

Staring back, the girl's black eyes were equally amazed. The Ohlone girl thought that she was dreaming. She believed the dream world had called up three odd humans. She wondered why the young ones were covered with dark, loose cloth. She wondered why there were heavy baskets attached to their feet.

As she came closer, the Ohlone girl stretched out her arms and smiled. It was a gesture of welcome to her dream. Then, she turned and beckoned them to follow.

"Should we go?" Maisha asked Misty Horn warily.

"As long as we've come this far, I think we should," he replied.

They walked along a marsh. The green-blue estuary

water—a combination of fresh water from the creeks and salt water from the bay—was filled with fish, frogs, grasses, sedge, and clusters of light, strong, tule rushes. The briny smell of the sea was powerful.

Before them was a huge hill. It was made of shells. When Europeans first saw these hills, they called them "shell mounds."

However, when the shell mounds were eventually dismantled, in addition to shells, there were skeletons, pottery, jewelry, and other artifacts inside them. Some scholars believe that the shell mounds were sacred and ceremonial. Others believe that they were refuse piles for the clams, oysters, and mussels that the Ohlone ate. The mystery of the shell mounds has never been solved.

To pass the giant shell mound, they had to walk a quarter of a mile. The Ohlone girl walked quickly. She was excited. Her vision dreams usually came in the early morning or late at night. Usually, only birds and fishes visited her in dreams.

Frequently, she turned around to see if her dream friends, with the strange skin, strange cloth, and strange baskets on their feet, still followed her. When she smiled at them, her bright white teeth flashed like mica in the sun.

Beyond the shell mound were the sounds of the village.

Pow! Powpow! Pow! Powpow!

It was the dynamic rhythm of pounding. In addition to the pounding, they also heard singing. Women's voices filled the air with song and laughter.

The village consisted of a few dozen round, or bun-shaped, huts. Situated between the green-blue marsh and the rocky shore, the huts were made of pale tule rushes, tied together with reeds. In the top of each hut was a hole for smoke to rise up and go out.

Next to the large residential huts were smaller storage huts, raised up on stilts. This was to keep the food supply—acorns, seeds, berries, dried meat, and dried fish—safe and dry. This was to keep their food away from animals.

Maisha and Mario stared at the Ohlone village. They were frightened. They did not know where they were. They did not know how they got there. They thought they were dreaming, too.

A small group of women was in view. The women wore heavy abalone shell coverings, tule aprons, and buckskin skirts. Cowry shells and feathers decorated their hair. Cowry earrings dangled from their ears. Tattoos zigzagged down their faces and arms.

Most of the women were pounding acorns. All of them were singing. A couple of women sat, weaving baskets with willow shoots, black fern roots, and tan-colored sedge. Their fingers moved quickly as they looped the materials into tiny stitches. It took thousands of stitches to make a basket. When it was finished, the basket would have an intricate design. It would be a work of art.

None of the women noticed the strangers. They did not look up from the mortars where they were crushing acorns or from their basket weaving.

The young Ohlone girl skipped over to the women. She shouted and pointed.

Finally, the women stopped singing. They looked up from their tasks. They looked where the girl pointed.

Then, they laughed and shook their heads. Soon, they returned to the work at hand: pounding acorns and making baskets.

From time to time, the Ohlone girl would tell the women in the village her dreams and visions. The people in the village believed this girl's visions were a sign of special powers. They believed that she would grow up to be a great healer. She would become a medicine woman who could cure the sick.

The Ohlone girl scooped a few handfuls of finely-ground acorn flour from her mother's mortar. She placed the scoops of flour into a basket and skipped back to Maisha, Mario, and Misty Horn.

Maisha gazed with wonder at the basket. The design was beautiful. It was a beautiful, perfect thing.

The Ohlone girl lifted her hand to her mouth. It was a gesture that asked her dream friends if they would like to eat.

In return, Misty Horn drew a line in the air. Not only did the line go to his mouth, but it tracked around his head and out to the sea.

The girl followed his hand with her intense black eyes. She understood. The friends in her dream wanted to eat whale or clams or eggs or fish with their acorn mush.

Out on the blue-gray bay were a few light, buoyant boats. The boats bobbed on the water. The Ohlone boats, like the huts, were made of tule bundles, tied together.

The sun had dropped in the west. The sky was golden. It was close to sunset.

The boats were returning to the village. As soon as the first boat landed on shore, the Ohlone girl skipped down to the water. She helped the men pull the boats onto the sand.

The men lifted out baskets of birds' eggs from a nearby island. The girl asked if she could have three eggs for her dream friends.

Although the men laughed, they took the girl's visions seriously. They believed in her visions. They believed they were a sign that someday the girl would gather herbs, bark, and roots for her medicine pouch. Someday, she would become a powerful healer or shaman.

The Ohlone girl carried the eggs in a willow basket, woven with a complicated diamond-shape design. Tonight, she would not eat with her mother, father, sisters, and brothers. Tonight, she would cook a special meal for her dream friends from faraway.

As she came closer, the Ohlone girl stretched out her arms and smiled.

Hello, Good-Bye

Maisha and Mario watched as the Ohlone girl made a fire. First, she placed dry leaves into a pile. She lay twigs and a couple of small logs beside the pile. She rubbed together two rocks. The rocks were flint. When rubbed together, the friction of the flint made a spark. As soon as the spark leapt onto the dry leaves, a small fire began to blaze.

The Ohlone girl put a smooth, oval-shaped river rock directly into the fire.

Maisha and Mario looked at each other with the same question: do Ohlones eat rocks as well as acorns?

Misty Horn interrupted the silence. "Are you enjoying yourselves?" he asked.

His voice startled them. The Ohlone girl's eyes grew larger, wider, darker, and more intense. No one in her dreams had ever spoken any language but Ohlone.

Misty Horn smiled kindly and traced another line in the air. His fingers pointed to the four directions: east, south, west, and north. To reassure her, he began to sing a lullaby:

Rock-a-bye baby in the treetop
When the wind blows, the cradle will rock.
When the wind blows, the cradle will fall
And down will come baby, cradle and all.

The Ohlone girl grinned with pleasure. Her head moved gently to the tune. She liked the sound of the strange, foreign words.

When the song was finished, she clapped her hands with delight. She hoped that he would sing it again. She hoped that she could remember the strange words.

The Ohlone girl stepped over to a creek that flowed down from the hills. She cupped her hands and put a small amount of water into the tightly woven basket. None of the water leaked from the basket. It was absolutely waterproof.

By now, the smooth rock in the fire glowed red with heat. With two sticks, she balanced and lifted the rock from the fire. She put it into the waterproof basket. Almost immediately, the water in the basket began to boil.

Maisha and Mario gazed at her with admiration.

Under her breath, Maisha said, "Cool."

"Way cool," Mario whispered.

They had never seen a basket that could hold boiling water. The girl added the eggs and boiled them for four minutes.

"Like us," Mario said.

After the eggs were cooked, she balanced them on sticks and removed them from the water. She now added acorn flour to the hot water and stirred it constantly to make a gruel or mush. When the mush was ready, she added smoked salmon.

It was time to eat.

The girl murmured in her own Ohlone language. "Thank you for the gift of this food," she said.

Although Maisha and Mario could not understand her words, they recognized the meaning. In their own homes, blessings on the food were also said. They knew that food was precious.

The Ohlone girl motioned for them to sit beside the basket and to take small portions with their fingers.

They had never eaten acorn mush. It was bland. It reminded Maisha of grits. It reminded Mario of *atole*. Maisha and Mario both wished they had honey, butter, and salt. However, when they mixed flakes of smoked salmon into the acorn concoction, it was tasty. They were content.

The Ohlone girl was content, too. She had heard a song from another world. She could recall one word: *tree-top*. She had fed her dream friends, and they had eaten. They chewed the food and swallowed. They ate like her people. They ate like the Ohlones.

Into the Fog

As the fishermen passed, they glimpsed three shadows next to the Ohlone girl. However, they did not stop. They were in a hurry. With burden baskets strapped to their heads, they were on their way to find a beached whale that they had spied from their boats. Later in the night, they would return with meat and blubber. The following day, the village would celebrate by eating whale.

Night enveloped them. Owls hooted. Coyotes howled. Countless stars twinkled in the sky. The air was perfectly fresh. It was hard to believe that they were in Richmond.

Mario held out his hand to touch the Ohlone girl. He wanted to see if she was real.

The girl surprised them. She hugged them. She hugged each one of her dream friends. Then, she gave them a string of cowry shells, an abalone that had been shaped and polished, and a whistle made of bird bones.

"Thank you," they said.

Maisha wished that she had something to give the girl in return. She searched the pockets of her hoodie where she found a few eucalyptus leaves.

The Ohlone girl touched the unfamiliar, brittle, aromatic leaves. The shape of the leaf was like the willow, but they did not smell like willow. The sharp, camphor smell of the leaves was from a tree that did not grow near her village. The tree did not yet grow anywhere in California or the western hemisphere. The tree was not a native species.

Again, they walked past the huge shell mound and along the shore towards the Ohlone village. As the fog enveloped them, Maisha asked, "Why are you named Misty?"

Misty Horn smiled. It was a story he liked to tell.

"My mother said I emerged from the mists of infinity. Although everything that lives must die, infinity goes on forever. All my life, I have looked for infinity in the tiniest grain of sand and in stars millions of light years away. My mother wanted me to be a seeker. She gave me a seeker's name."

Since they had traveled back in time, Maisha better understood the way that Misty Horn spoke and the mysterious things he said.

Close to the village, the wind picked up. It was a cool wind, blowing into the bay from the ocean in the west. Whitecaps danced on top of the waves. The wind blew harder and whipped the water into a white froth. It mowed down the tule rushes and grasses in the marsh. Clouds of fog and mist raced across the moon.

The wind became so fierce that Maisha and Mario were forced to close their eyes. When they opened them, the Ohlone girl and village had vanished.

They were no longer walking on a path. Instead, they stood beside a straight dirt road that bordered a marshland on one side and wheat fields on the other. In the distance, lights glowed softly. Farther away, factory smokestacks spewed large orange flames.

"Where are we?" Mario asked.

"Richmond," Misty Horn winked his bluish-brown eye.

"I've never been to this part of town," Mario said.

"We're near Nystrom School. Macdonald Avenue is not far."

"I go to Nystrom," Maisha said, looking around. "There's no marsh. The street isn't dirt. Cars and trucks pass day and night."

"There's no marsh by Lincoln School either," Mario nodded.

Misty Horn waved his hands through the air. Although he knew they were in Richmond, he was unsure of the year. The shell mound, one of the largest on the bay, was still visible. That meant it was not yet 1917 when the shell mound was removed.

Maisha searched for a landmark. They passed a large clapboard house with a fenced garden. They passed a barn and barnyard with horses and cows. They passed a horse and buggy with a sleepy driver. She recognized nothing.

"These are some of the original lines of the Iron Triangle," Misty Horn said, as they stepped across a railroad track.

"Trains, traveling from faraway, stopped in Richmond. Everyday, the Southern Pacific ran eighty trains in and out of a station over at Sixteenth and Macdonald. The Atchison, Topeka, and Santa Fe had separate tracks, trains, train yards, and machine shops. Crude oil was piped three-hundred miles from southern California, stored in a 'tank farm' in San Pablo, and then brought to the refinery where it was shipped out. You see, Richmond's deep shoreline water made it the perfect junction for rail, oil, and ships on the Pacific coast. There was even a whaling station at Point Molate, but you'll have to wait a few decades for that."

Mario and Maisha knew about the trains in Richmond. They heard them blow their loud whistles everyday. They knew about the oil in Richmond. Sometimes, they smelled the foul fumes from the refineries. Whales, however, were a big surprise.

Mario wanted to ask more about the whaling station, but they had reached a campfire. The silhouettes of seven men emerged in the fog. The men sat silently beside a fire, smoking long, hand-rolled cigarettes and throwing dice on the damp, bare ground. They wore long black robes and quilted black jackets. Their shiny dark hair was plaited in a braid down their backs.

"Lost?" one of them asked with a strong accent.

"Not lost," Misty Horn calmly replied. "Just going home."

The men appeared nervous. They swept the dice out of sight. They folded their arms across their chests. They kept their eyes down.

"Good-night," Misty Horn said, guiding Mario and Maisha away from the campfire.

However, after a couple of steps, two men seized Mario's baggy jeans and dragged him close to the light of the fire.

"Montoya boy," one declared, peering into Mario's face.

"Me?" Mario trembled.

"Tell father, get money," he said to Misty Horn.

"My papá?" Mario asked in confusion.

"Montoya no pay!"

Misty Horn, old as he was, tugged on Mario's arm. He pulled hard in the opposite direction, but the Chinese man held fast.

"You have made a serious mistake," Misty Horn reasoned.

"You tell father, he pay us now. He owe us money. You tell father, we got his boy."

Maisha began to cry. She could clearly see that these were angry men. She knew about anger. It made people dangerous. Whenever she saw an angry person, she got out of their way.

"He doesn't live here," she pleaded as the tears rolled down her cheeks.

"He live here," the Chinese man said. "He live on big ranch by San Pablo."

"Ranch?" Maisha blurted. "There are no ranches."

Maisha tried to see into the fog. Up and down the empty dirt street, she searched for a patrol car. There were no cars in sight. There was no public telephone to call 9-1-1. There were only a couple of nearby houses, both shuttered and dark.

Mario tried to loosen the men's grip from his wrists. He thought that he could run away and hide inside the fog. Although small and emaciated, the men were extremely strong.

"Get father," the boss ordered Misty Horn.

"Wrong boy," Misty Horn argued.

"Get Montoya quick," he repeated. Then, he made a deadly gesture. He drew a finger across his throat, as if he meant to cut Mario.

Thieves in the Night

"During the mid-1800s, thousands of immigrants came from China to California to work in the gold mines and on the railroads. After the mines closed and the railroads were mostly built, many Chinese worked at the shrimp camps on the Richmond coast. They worked in the dangerous dynamite factories on Giant Road," Misty Horn explained in a whisper.

"Often, the Chinese were used and abused. People took advantage of the immigrants. Sometimes, they did not get paid for their work. Sometimes, they were forced to work for free," he continued.

"The California government passed discrimination laws, restricting the Chinese. There was extreme prejudice against them in California, similar to the Jim Crow laws against blacks in the southern United States."

"But it isn't Mario's fault," Maisha cried. "Mario wasn't even born."

"Get Montoya quick," the man repeated as he yanked Mario's arms and tied them behind him.

"I'll get help," Maisha said in a panic.

"Don't leave!" Misty Horn commanded. "We must stay together, no matter what!"

Despite the warning, Maisha ran towards Macdonald Avenue. Behind her, she heard Misty Horn calling, "Maisha, come back! Maisha, you may not find us again! We have to stick together! Maisha! Maisha!"

A wagon emerged from the fog. Harnessed to the wagon was a team of four mules, steadily pulling a wide and heavy load. Seated on a board were three rough men.

"Hello!" Maisha waved frantically.

The trio stared at the veil of fog where the outline of a child emerged. They were not happy to see *or* be seen by anyone. They were thieves. They had been paid to steal a wooden shack off its brick pilings in Point Richmond, put it on a wagon, and deliver it to an empty field on the east side of Macdonald Avenue.

The wealthy gentleman, who hired them, told the men, "Sneak the shack out on a foggy night at a late hour. If you get caught by the authorities, I shall pretend to know nothing about it."

As it turned out, they were stealing a United States post-office!

"She don't resemble no authority," the wagon driver said, spitting his plug of tobacco into the mud.

"She's a little colored girl," another observed, watching Maisha wave and race towards them.

"What's a little colored girl doing around at this hour?" the third man asked.

"Must be one of them feeble-minded children who got loose somehow."

"Colored people don't live around here."

"Maybe, she ain't colored. Maybe, she's Californio or Italiano or Portuguese."

"She ain't none of them," the driver of the wagon stated. "She's colored."

Maisha was panting when she reached the wagon. She leaned into its side to catch her breath.

"Get home," the men whispered harshly.

"Can't you see we working?" the driver growled.

"Sorry, sir," Maisha apologized. "Please, can you tell me where to call 9-1-1?"

The men turned to each other. "Ain't never heard of it."

"I need the number," Maisha stuttered, "for the police."

She scanned the men's dirty faces. Their beady eyes were hard and unforgiving. Their grizzled beards were long and uncombed. They wore bib overalls and wide-brimmed hats, pulled low across their foreheads. Her sixth sense told her that they were not trustworthy, but Maisha had no one else to ask.

"Maybe you can call the police for me," she begged.

"Policeman is about the last person we call tonight," the driver said gruffly.

"But there's an emergency in the China camp," Maisha continued.

"What we care about them?" the driver snarled. "We don't care a rat's tail about them."

Then, the driver lifted his mule whip and flicked it at Maisha. The tip of the leather thong grazed her cheek. It stung. It stung painfully.

Maisha touched her face. She could feel a trickle of warm, sticky blood where the whip had cut her.

"You holding up important business here," the driver said. "I ain't aiming to hurt you again, but you got to get out of our way."

He held the whip, poised in the air. "If we hear about you telling a soul what you seen, we come and find you," he added furiously.

Richmond's Newspapers

As Maisha ran, occasionally the fog lifted. In the distance, she could see factories and fiery smokestacks. On either side of Macdonald Avenue were brick and wooden structures. In between the buildings were empty fields where the muddy earth was plowed under, ready for planting.

She wondered if Misty Horn were wrong. She wondered if she were really in Richmond. On the sidewalk was a newspaper whose banner read:

Her mouth fell open. "What in the world!" she gasped. Nineteen-hundred-and-fifteen was almost a hundred years ago!

On the front pages were photographs of an enormous factory, constructed of light-colored brick. The interior of the factory was filled with the famous Pullman sleeping cars under repair. Each car was like a small dormitory where passengers could lie down and sleep while traveling long distances by train.

The headline read:

The Pullman Company Celebrates Five Years in Richmond: Pullman Prophecies Fulfilled

There was also a photo of Standard Oil Refinery's mile-long loading pier.

**Thousands of Men Work Day and Night,
Seven Days a Week, to Send
Standard's Refined Oil
to the Four Corners of the World**

Another picture showed a family beside a trolley. The girls wore hats and pinafores and short, laced boots. The boy wore knickers and a driving cap.

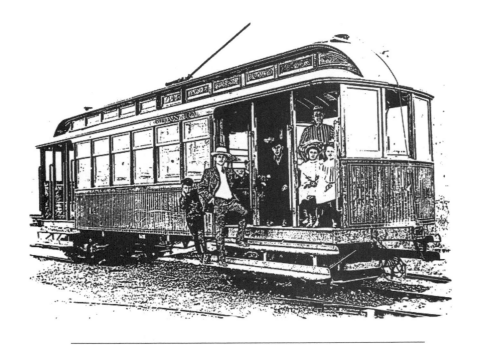

Dr. Edmund Forsyth of Richmond and His Family Take Electric Trolley to Attend Berkeley Football Game
GO BEARS!

On the backside of the paper was an announcement of a meeting of the Northern California chapter of the

N.A.A.C.P. It also included news of their boycott of the new film, *Birth of a Nation.*

Maisha knew that N.A.A.C.P. was the acronym for National Association for the Advancement of Colored People. She also knew that it was one of the first Civil Rights organizations in America. It was a surprise, however, to learn that the N.A.A.C.P. was older than Auntie Yates herself.

There were advertisements for Italian grocery companies, a match factory, rooming houses, wine from Winehaven, a roofing company, and real estate lots for sale by Augustin S. Macdonald.

Maisha raced on, finally passing a couple of familiar landmarks. She recognized the yellowish brick First National Bank building at the corner of Sixth and Macdonald. She recognized another building that in 1915 served as a market, a bar, and a hotel. In fact, these blocks of the Iron Triangle looked like the prosperous center of a small, prosperous city.

When she finally reached a light at the end of Sixth Street, she stared in awe at the wooden sign. "Barrett Avenue! That's where I live!" she exclaimed.

Instead of apartment complexes, Laundromats, and corner markets, there was a block of narrow brick and wooden houses. Over the door of **Wanske's Saloon**, one light shone. However, the ramshackle bar was locked up. A sign—*COME AGAIN*—swung from the porch railing.

Gathering her courage, Maisha knocked.

"Wanske is closed!" a man yelled from a basement window next door. "Can't you idiots read?"

Maisha turned to the open window and the loud, annoyed voice.

"I'm looking for the police," she said urgently.

"Shouldn't you be home in bed?" the invisible man asked in a softer tone.

"I guess I'm lost," Maisha confessed.

"I should say so," he agreed, poking his white, bushy head out the window. "Push open the front door and come down. At least, you can warm yourself."

Holding onto the wobbly banister, Maisha descended a long set of rickety stairs. Overhead, a single light bulb hung from a string to light the way. When she reached the basement, six inches of water stood on the floor. Planks, balanced on bricks, straddled the flooded area.

At the far end of the basement was a open door marked: *Daily News*. She stepped over the threshold. The floor of the office was also covered in water and crisscrossed with wooden planks.

Several feet above the ground stood a big machine with cranks, pulleys, rollers, wheels, levers, and a keyboard. Cast-iron molds of letter forms, or matrices, in different shapes and sizes were stacked on shelves along the wall. Large vats of ink balanced on brick piers. The strong, pleasing smell of newsprint competed with the awful smell of mold.

A man with an enormous face and long white muttonchop whiskers stood by the printing press.

"Welcome to the *Daily News*," he said cordially.

The man's shirt sleeves were rolled up with garters. His tweed vest was unbuttoned. His hands were streaked with black ink. An unlit cigar hung from the corner of his mouth. Most noticeable of all were the tall, thigh-high, rubber wading boots that allowed him to walk around in several inches of water.

Removing the cigar, he added, "I'm just finishing the press run for tomorrow's edition."

"I hoped you were the police," Maisha sighed.

The man laughed so hard that all the fat in his face jiggled.

"Afraid not," he replied, sticking out his hand. "My name is Daniel Duggle. I run the *Daily News*. We cover working-man news for working men around the world.

Richmond is a town of working men. I didn't start in Richmond, but I'm here now. When I began a career in the news business, Richmond hardly existed. There were only 200 people in 1900. Now, it's a metropolis of 15,000!"

Maisha stood on a chair, watching Mr. Duggle maneuver the crank that turned a large rolling drum or platen. When sheets of newspaper came off the drum, he picked them off at the moist corners and placed them under heat lamps to dry.

"I covered the economic Panic of 1893, the Spanish-American War, the assassination of President McKinley, the victory of the eight-hour work day, the Great Quake of 1906, and of course, the Panama-Pacific International Expo. I bet you liked going to that," he grinned.

"I didn't go," Maisha admitted shyly.

"Eighteen million people visited San Francisco's Expo this year, and you missed it! You missed air shows, submarines, reindeer, a replica of the Panama Canal, and a forty-three story Tower of Jewels!"

Breathless, Mr. Duggle stuck the cigar back into his mouth.

"I'm afraid I've just arrived," Maisha apologized, holding up the mud-splattered newspaper.

"That's my biggest rival," Daniel Duggle laughed heartily. "Here in Richmond, we have several daily papers and weeklies, too. There's lots of news in a growing town like Richmond or as some like to call it, *The Wonder City.*"

"I found this paper in the street," Maisha said.

"That's not all you found," Mr. Duggle observed, spying the nasty cut on her cheek.

"It's nothing," Maisha said, feeling braver than usual.

"We wouldn't want it to turn septic."

Maisha was unfamiliar with the word, but Daniel Duggle's tone made it sound horrible. He reached for a First Aid box on his cluttered desk. He took out a cotton swab, a bottle of rubbing alcohol, and a vial of iodine. First, he applied the icy liquid to the cut. Next, he dabbed it with the orange antiseptic.

"I know it stings," he said, blowing on her cheek.

Maisha bit her lip to keep from howling.

"What happened?"

"It doesn't matter," Maisha said. "What matters are my friends. I have to find help."

"Is that what brings you out at this hour?" he asked, checking the flat gold watch in his vest pocket.

Maisha tried to untangle the story: the angry men at the campfire and their mistaking Mario for Mr. Montoya's son. As she explained the desperate situation, tears welled up in her eyes.

"This sounds like a case of kidnaping," Mr. Duggle said. "Let's start at the beginning. In the newspaper business, I'm required to ask you five essential questions."

A Ride in Lizzie

Maisha had no time for questions. "I have to go," she panicked.

"I can help," Mr. Duggle offered kindly. "If we take Lizzie, it'll be much quicker than going by foot."

"Are you sure?" Maisha asked, guessing that Lizzie must be Mr. Duggle's fastest horse.

"Mind? This is an important scoop for my newspaper. Kidnaping or worse deserves a special afternoon edition."

"Worse?" Maisha cried.

She could imagine nothing worse. However, she was glad to have Daniel Duggle as an ally. She followed him across the flooded basement, up the steps, and into the backyard of *Wanske's Saloon*.

Mr. Duggle unlocked the doors of a weatherbeaten barn. Inside, Maisha expected to see horses, but instead, there was a shiny, old automobile.

Actually, it was a new automobile although it looked old to Maisha. It was a Ford Model-T or "Tin Lizzie," as it was affectionately called. Maisha inspected the tall, black, boxy contraption. There was a whitewall tire mounted on its rear. In fact, all the tires were wide whitewalls with heavy spokes that appeared more suitable for bicycles than cars.

"Get into Lizzie," Mr. Duggle said, removing his rubber wading boots and slipping into shoes.

Maisha stepped on the running board and climbed onto the leather seat. Through the large front windshield, she could see the fog lifting. A few stars twinkled in the black sky.

She gazed at the stars. She thought how these same stars had shone for countless years. They had shone in Ohlone time. They had shone in 1915. They had shone on Barrett Avenue where her mother waited for her to come home. They had shone over her daddy in Texas. They had shone on Auntie Yates' garden in North Richmond. The stars made Maisha feel connected to everyone.

"Mario, don't worry," she murmured softly to herself. "I'm getting help."

Mr. Duggle turned a crank on the outside of the car. After a few turns, Lizzie burst into life with a spurt, a sputter, and a jolt.

He slid onto the seat beside Maisha. He reached into the back and pulled out a mohair blanket which he laid across her lap. He put on a big checkered cap and a pair of leather mesh driving gloves that buttoned at the wrist.

"It gets as chilly as an ice cone in here," Mr. Duggle warned. "Once we get going twenty miles per hour, you'll start to freeze."

"Is that as fast it goes?" Maisha asked skeptically. Even her daddy's half-broken truck went faster by twice as much.

"On a good day, I can push it up to 35 mph. It runs on gasoline, you know," he boasted.

"Don't all automobiles run on gasoline?" she asked.

"My first one ran on steam," Mr. Duggle replied. "Steam, electric, gas, they make all kinds of vehicles."

Mr. Duggle put the Tin Lizzie into gear. It jerked forward a few feet and stopped. He got out of the car and cranked it again. It moved a few more feet across the yard.

"I'd better walk," Maisha said, lifting the handle of the door.

"It's too far to walk," Daniel Duggle cautioned. "The police station is at Point Richmond. The Montoya place is near Tank Hill."

"It gets as chilly as an ice cone in here,"
Mr. Duggle warned.

Again, Lizzie was cranked and again, it stalled. Finally, the car leapt forward at a slow but steady pace.

"Okay, let's go find your friends!" Mr. Duggle exclaimed as he lit his cigar and took hold of the steering wheel. "Maybe I can talk some sense into those fellows and help them get paid."

"Do you mind not smoking?" Maisha asked quietly.

No one had ever asked Daniel Duggle not to smoke, but he obliged by stubbing out the cigar in the ashtray.

"Which direction?" He looked to her for guidance.

Maisha turned her eyes forward and back, left and right, up and down. She pointed towards Macdonald Avenue. "I'm certain there was a field."

"There are fields everywhere in Richmond," Mr. Duggle commented.

"There were also a couple of large houses with big porches and railroad tracks nearby."

"That's not helpful either," Daniel Duggle said. "Trains from across the country pass through Richmond. There are so many trains everyday and so many tracks that they named this part of town the *Iron Triangle*."

"I already know that! What I need to figure out is where the Chinese people stay."

Mr. Duggle thoughtfully stroked his double chin.

"They used to live in the shrimp camps at Point Molate and out by the dynamite plants. You couldn't have walked that far."

"It was a short walk," she confirmed. "I'm sure it's only a few blocks away."

"Don't worry. We'll take a swing around town and try to find your friends."

Maisha snuggled under the blanket as they puttered down Macdonald Avenue. They cruised past the new City Hall at Twentieth and Maine and out Twenty-third Street to Cutting Boulevard and Pullman Avenue, passing buggies harnessed with horses and wagons pulled by mules. Occasionally, a single rider on horseback would trot by and wave.

Maisha's eyes roamed from one side of the road to the other, searching for campfires. "What's that huge hill?" she asked.

"They call it Easter Hill," Mr. Duggle said.

"But they took down the hill!" Maisha exclaimed.

"Took it down? It's right in front of your nose. If you want, I can stop Lizzie so you can touch it."

"It's too hard to explain, Mr. Duggle."

"I guess you've never been to this part of town," he said.

"I guess I haven't," Maisha agreed.

The Californios of California

The fog drifted towards Oak Grove, the old name for El Sobrante. Bright against the velvet-black sky hung the full moon like a globe.

Esteban Montoya had built his house and ranch on the west end of the family's original land grant. This tract of land had been given to his grandfather before the late 1840s when Mexico lost control of Alta California and the southwestern United States.

Like most Spaniards and Mexicans who settled in Upper California, Esteban Montoya called himself a "Californio." He had Spanish roots, the Spanish language, and Spanish culture, but he no longer considered himself Spanish or Mexican. California was his home.

Mr. Duggle stopped the car on the pebble driveway that surrounded the dark, two-story house. In the center of the drive was a tile fountain spouting a jet of water. Two large palm trees stood symmetrically on either side of a massive front door.

"Guess we'll have to wake somebody up," he said.

"Do you know them?" Maisha inquired.

"I wrote a news story about his uncles' squabbles over the rancho. He didn't appreciate my stirring up the family's hornet's nest."

Daniel Duggle lifted the big, brass doorknocker. When the knocker dropped, a boom echoed across the yard, followed by a graveyard silence.

Beyond the yard were rolling hills. In contrast to the Ohlone times, most of the hillsides had been logged and were now bare of old-growth trees.

Across Montoya's fields, rows of tall eucalyptus trees had been planted as windbreaks. Since Ohlone times, the eucalyptus had been imported from Australia to California. Now, they grew all over the state.

Nearby, Maisha spied Tank Hill that housed Standard's crude oil. It looked exactly like a flat footprint of Hilltop Mall. She knew exactly where she was.

Mr. Duggle dropped the doorknocker again. Three times, he banged it. Three times, it reverberated into the darkness.

Slowly, one of the heavy doors swung back. *"Si?"* a boy asked, gazing up. He held a candelabra with five lit candles.

"Is your father here?" Mr. Duggle asked him.

"He's not here, sir," the boy said.

"Your mother?" Mr. Duggle inquired.

Several small boys and girls crowded in the doorway. They had crawled out of their warm beds to investigate.

"We're here, señor," the youngest child piped up, rubbing his sleepy eyes.

"I must have an immediate word with your father," Mr. Duggle insisted.

"He's at Ferry Point," the eldest boy replied. "He and my mother went to meet my grandmother. She is coming to visit for Thanksgiving."

"Thank you, sonny," Mr. Duggle touched the brim of his driving cap. "Sorry to disturb the family."

As the boy started to shut the door, Maisha jumped from the automobile.

"He looks exactly like my friend!" she cried. "He looks exactly like Mario!"

The boy stared at the strange-looking girl in boy's pants. "Who looks like me?" he asked.

"My friend, Mario Reyes," Maisha said. "He was kidnaped tonight. We think they mistook him for you."

Enrico Montoya visibly shuddered. His family was rich. Sometimes, he worried that a kidnapper might prey on him and his siblings.

"You mean, someone wanted to kidnap me?" he stam-mered.

"If anyone else comes here tonight, do not let them in," Daniel Duggle advised. "We're heading to Ferry Point."

Ferry Point

The trip to Ferry Point in Lizzie was slow. Only some of the route was paved. Recent rains had turned the dirt roads to mud. Mr. Duggle had to drive cautiously to avoid the deep ruts. They passed a couple of cars, stalled deep in the mire, as well as an abandoned wagon, stuck in the muddy tracks.

In 1915, two tunnels connected Point Richmond to Ferry Point: a Santa Fe train tunnel with tracks; and a truck and automobile tunnel, also used by wagons and buggies.

During the day, Ferry Point bustled with commuters, traveling back and forth to San Francisco. From Point Castro, there was also a new ferry service that traveled to San Rafael. In fact in 1915, fifty ferries operated around San Francisco Bay, more than any other place in the world.

When Lizzie emerged from the tunnel, Mr. Duggle chose to park on a small promontory with a view of Ferry

Point, Mount Tamalpais, the humps of dark islands, and the beautiful San Francisco Bay. He removed a pair of binoculars from their case to scan the horizon.

"Do you see Mr. Montoya?" Maisha asked, peering at a group of friends and family outside the long terminal shed.

Daniel Duggle swiveled his binoculars back and forth. Bundled in large coats, capes, and hats, it was difficult to tell one person from the other.

"Montoya may have gone inside the waiting room," he said. "It's a bit chilly to stand and wait."

Maisha herself shivered with cold as she anxiously looked about her. It had been over an hour since she had last seen Mario.

"Let's hope your friend hasn't been Shanghaied," Mr. Duggle said soberly.

"'Shanghaied?'" Maisha asked with alarm. *That* sounded like a tragic fate.

"Ever hear of the city of Shanghai?" Mr. Duggle pointed to the gap between San Francisco and the tip of Marin County.

"There's no bridge!" Maisha gasped.

"Of course, there's no bridge," he confirmed. "The genius hasn't been born who can build a bridge there.

Maybe, a designer like Joseph Strauss could conceive it, but construction would be impossible."

Maisha remained silent. She did not want to stir up Mr. Duggle's curiosity by telling him that a world-famous bridge, called the Golden Gate, would be completed in 1937, only a little more than twenty years from today.

"If you sail through that gap," he continued, "you're in the Pacific Ocean, right? Hold a steady course west, and you'll reach Shanghai in about a month."

"A month!" Maisha exclaimed.

"It's over 6,000 miles. Once you are on the ship, there's no getting off. That's what 'shanghaiing' means. If they get you onboard, you're stuck until you reach China."

"Would they really do that to Mario?" Maisha cried.

"He's a strong, young lad. Am I right?"

Reluctantly, she agreed.

"There's no end of things for a lad to do on a ship. A boy like Mario could perform many chores."

Although Maisha told herself she had to stay strong for Mario, she buried her face in her hoodie and sobbed.

"Look!" Mr. Duggle nudged her shoulder and passed her the binoculars.

Maisha stared at the two tunnels that led in and out of Ferry Point. Emerging from one dark keyhole were seven men in long, black robes with long, black braids. They were dragging a boy by his ear. His hands were tied behind his back. A moment later, an old man also stumbled out of the tunnel.

"Your friends, I presume?" Mr. Duggle's bushy eyebrows rose in a question.

"Yes, my friends!" Maisha hugged Daniel Duggle with relief. "I'm going to them."

"Hold on," he grabbed her sleeve.

"But they're hurting Mario," she protested.

"We can't do anything without a plan, right?"

Maisha nodded solemnly.

"You reported that these men are angry. They haven't been paid. They've been mistreated. They're going to be mistrustful. We certainly don't want to anger them more."

With Mario in tow, they crept into the shadows of an overhanging rock. Panting for breath, an unhappy Misty Horn shuffled along and disappeared in the shadows, too.

With Mario in tow, they crept into the shadows
of an overhanging rock.

Confrontation at the Dock

Daniel Duggle handed paper and a pen over to Maisha. "For taking notes," he said.

"But I've never recorded a conversation," she stuttered.

"Just let me do the talking. You jot down the keywords."

"Like what?" Maisha asked.

"Keywords are the important words. They jump out at you. Later, I shall use your notes to write the story and give you a credit as my cub reporter."

Maisha's heart thumped with excitement.

"Ready?" he asked.

She uncapped the ink pen and carefully wrote at the top of the paper:

November 23, 1915, Ferry Point, Richmond, California

On San Francisco Bay, the *Santa Clara* steamed towards land. The moon splashed across the bow of the large, graceful, double-decker ferry. Its whistle blew loudly as it reduced its speed and glided into port.

Family and friends left the waiting room in the terminal shed and moved onto the dock. They waved hats and handkerchiefs at the passengers on the ferry's deck. Passengers waved scarves and handkerchiefs, too.

Walking briskly, Daniel Duggle and Maisha quickly reached the end of the dock and joined the others.

"Mr. Montoya?" Mr. Duggle tapped the back of a tall and elegantly dressed man in a bowler hat.

"Yes?" Esteban Montoya turned around. He removed an expensive, thin cigar from his mouth and smiled. "Are we acquainted?"

"I am Daniel Duggle from the *Daily News*," Mr. Duggle said, extending his hand.

"You'll have to excuse me," Mr. Montoya replied curtly. "I do not talk to reporters."

He took his wife's arm. Together, they pressed through the crowd to get closer to the prow of the *Santa Clara*.

The ferry's crew cast mooring ropes around the iron supports by the pier. A gate in the ship's railing swung back. The walkway was lowered.

Like all good reporters, Daniel Duggle was extremely persistent. "I'm afraid I have to interrupt your family reunion," he said, tapping Esteban Montoya's back again.

"Can't this wait until a civilized hour?" An annoyed Mr. Montoya lost his patience.

"I'm afraid it cannot wait. I've already been to your home this evening, hoping you might resolve a piece of urgent business."

"My home?" Mr. Montoya shouted. "You awoke my children?"

"Your children may be in danger." Mr. Duggle's words hit their target.

"What danger?" Mrs. Montoya cried.

"It's nothing," Mr. Montoya said, moving away from Daniel Duggle. "He's a pesky reporter."

"What danger?" she repeated apprehensively.

Mr. Duggle pointed to an overhanging rock in the distance. "There's a boy there who bears an uncanny resemblance to your eldest son, Enrico."

Furious, Mr. Montoya interrupted, "Tell me, sir, how does that concern us?"

Maisha, who was quickly taking notes, stopped scribbling. She looked up at Mr. Montoya and blurted, "My friend wouldn't be in a mess if you had properly paid your workers."

Daniel Duggle nodded in agreement. However, his stern expression reminded Maisha that he, *not she*, was talking.

Ignoring Mr. Duggle, Maisha charged ahead. "You took advantage of seven Chinese immigrants."

"Esteban!" Hortensia Montoya fiercely whispered to her husband. "Do something."

"Please get her away from me immediately," Mr. Montoya pointed to Maisha. "Or I shall ask the ferry captain to call the police."

"Excellent idea," Maisha smiled slyly.

"The workers of Richmond won't take kindly to this news," Mr. Duggle remarked.

"Are you threatening me?" Esteban Montoya fumed.

"I can see it now," Mr. Duggle said, positioning his forefinger and thumb as if he were reading a headline:

Innocent Boy Held for Unpaid Wages!

Mrs. Montoya stepped up to Mr. Duggle. She shoved her husband away. She opened her beaded bag. "How much does Señor Montoya owe them?"

"Hortensia! Don't you dare converse with this Duggle man!"

Hortensia Montoya gave her husband a withering look.

"Please, do not advise me," she snapped. "You have endangered our children with your questionable conduct."

The Reunion

Señora Montoya buckled the clasps of her fur cape. She tilted her fashionable, winged hat. She grasped the ivory knob of her silk umbrella. Then, she turned and marched off the pier, away from her husband and the *Santa Clara*.

Daniel Duggle and Maisha followed closely behind her.

"It's a little far to walk. It's muddy, too. Why don't I drive us?" Mr. Duggle offered.

Hortensia Montoya climbed into Lizzie. When they reached the rocky overhang, Daniel Duggle stopped the car.

Two familiar voices shouted, "Maisha! Maisha!"

She started to run, but Mr. Duggle firmly held her back and whispered, "No sudden moves!"

Bundled in a quilt jacket, a Chinese man emerged

from the shadows. He stood silently beside Lizzie, neither speaking nor smiling.

"I shall pay you," Hortensia Montoya said to him, opening her dainty purse.

The leader shouted something in Chinese to the other men. Immediately, Misty Horn emerged from the shadows. He embraced Maisha and pumped Mr. Duggle's hand. "I can't thank you enough for finding this child."

"On the contrary," Daniel Duggle replied. "It's Maisha Yates who found me."

"Whatever," Misty Horn sighed with relief. "I was distressed to think I would lose her to an entirely different century."

Mr. Duggle shot him a puzzled look, but Maisha grinned and said, "Here I am."

Mario staggered forward. He was pale. His ear was swollen and bloody. However, Maisha had never seen anyone look as happy as Mario Reyes at that moment.

He raised two fingers in the peace sign and cried out, "You rock, Maisha Yates!"

Hortensia Montoya blanched. Although the youth was dressed in peculiar and ill-fitting clothes, he was a twin of her Enrico.

"Enrico," she murmured, knowing these men could have taken the right boy instead of the wrong one.

The account was soon settled: sixty cents per day for each of the seven men, multiplied by five days of work. The bills and coins were distributed. With their pay in hand, the men ran back into the Ferry Point tunnel.

Hortensia Montoya returned to her husband and mother-in-law beside the *Santa Clara*. Mr. Duggle also excused himself. With Maisha's notes in hand, he headed off to write a special edition of the kidnaping and rescue of Mario Reyes: *a tale that could have ended tragically except for the persistence of young cub reporter, Maisha Yates, and the upstanding moral conscience of Hortensia Montoya.*

All alone, Mario, Maisha, and Misty Horn huddled by the dock at Ferry Point. A wind began to blow from the west to the east. It blew in billows of chilly fog. Soon, the land, the hills, the ferry, and the sky were shrouded in thick mist. The wind blew so hard that they had to close their eyes. Tightly, they held each other's hands for fear of being separated again.

PART III

THEN, NOW, & LATER

Newsreels

Maisha awoke refreshed, as if she had been sleeping for a long, long time. However, she wasn't at home in her cozy bed. She was slumped in a chair in a large, dark, cavernous place. Sconces with soft lights lined the walls. Tiny fake stars sparkled on the black ceiling. In the distance, gray-and-white images of ships, bombs, fighter planes, and tanks flickered on a screen.

To Maisha's left was Misty Horn. His head was tilted back. His mouth was open. He was quietly snoring. On the other side of her was Mario. She inspected his swollen ear and the pimples on his forehead. Off and on, his eyelids twitched as he mumbled, "I'm not Enrico. I'm not Enrico Montoya."

She was in a crowded movie theater, but no one was watching the screen. All around her were scores of sleeping men.

Meanwhile, the screen images kept rapidly changing.

Each image was emboldened by a large headline and an announcer's deep voice. It was a newsreel of war and world events. Maisha was surprised to see Park Florist at 2015 Macdonald Avenue in Richmond, California on the screen. She recognized the street, but at the same time, she didn't recognize it. The frame of the film was filled with people, cars, buses, sailors, and soldiers, all from a different era in time.

Again, the newsreel voice reverberated in the movie house:

OUSTER OF ALL JAPS IN CALIFORNIA NEAR!
General DeWitt Rids the Area of Enemy Aliens!
Japs Sent to Camps!
Italians and Germans Forced to Move!

EXECUTIVE ORDER NO. 9066

FEBRUARY 19, 1942

Authorizing the Secretary of War to Prescribe Military Areas

Whereas, The successful prosecution of the war requires every possible protection against espionage and against sabotage to national defense material, national defense premises and national defense utilities as defined in Section 4, Act of April 20, 1918, 40 Stat. 533 as amended by the Act of November 30, 1940, 54 Stat. 1220. and the Act of August 21, 1941. 55 Stat. 655 (U.S.C., Title 50, Sec. 104):

Now, therefore, by virtue of the authority vested in me as President of the United States, and Commander in Chief of the Army and Navy, 1 hereby authorized and direct the Secretary of War, and the Military Commanders whom he may from time to time designate, whenever he or any designated

There was a film of Richmond's Japanese-American families, standing beside their cardboard boxes, bundles, and suitcases, stuffed with linens, clothing, and kitchenware. Everyone was nicely dressed in suits and hats, but the women and children were crying. A man held a sign: I AM AN AMERICAN!

The film rolled to Richmond's large Greyhound station on Twenty-third Street. Soldiers with guns and bayonets stood guard as Richmond's Japanese-Americans were herded onto a bus and rode off to an unknown destination.

Misty Horn's eyes opened and slowly adjusted to the darkness. Immediately, he recognized the interior of the Fox California movie theater in downtown Richmond.

"The war," he grimaced. "It must be spring 1942, the year our government sent our fellow citizens off to camps."

"Like the Nazis?" Maisha stammered. She had read *The Diary of Anne Frank*. She knew that the Nazis murdered millions of Jews and others in concentration camps. However, she never knew that American families were forced to go away to camps.

Misty Horn's head shook sadly. "The U.S. didn't kill them wholesale, but many Japanese-American families lost their businesses, their homes, and their health. Although kind neighbors saved some farms and houses, at the end of the war, others had nothing left. There are lots of ways to kill a human being."

"But I know Japanese people in Richmond," Maisha said.

"Of course, you do. People from all over the world live in Richmond. The Chinese and Japanese helped build California, but during the war, people with Japanese blood were treated cruelly. They were sent far away to camps. Germans and Italians were treated badly, too, and had to move away from the coast. Some of them also lost homes and businesses. With the Italian fishermen banished, we didn't have much fish to eat for a few years."

"But if they were American?" Maisha reasoned.

"Everyone was afraid that the Japanese would attack California. They believed their decent Japanese neighbors were their enemies," Misty Horn said bitterly. "You probably know that fear can warp good judgment. It turns men into monsters."

Maisha thought about her mother's wise words: *it's bad for the heart to live in fear.* She missed her mother terribly. She wanted to return to her Richmond.

"Do you think we can go back soon?" she asked.

"Soon," Misty Horn promised. "But as long as we're here, let's look around. Richmond is an entirely different place. It's a real boomtown."

The war newsreels ended. The feature *Bambi* began.

"Wake up Mario," Misty Horn suggested. "We'll go put something in our bellies."

"Mario!" Maisha whispered loudly.

In response, a dozen men groaned, moaned, snorted, and snored.

"Keep your voice down, toots!" one shouted.

"I'm asleep!" another yelled.

Mario shifted in his seat. He stretched his arms and opened one eye. "Where are we?" he grumbled.

"Cool your chords unless you want the taste of a knuckle sandwich!" a man roared.

"Come along," Misty Horn said, lifting Mario by the elbow and climbing over a row of sleeping men.

No Pancakes for Mario

Outside the movie theater, Mario and Maisha were dazzled by the commotion. Misty Horn was absolutely right. Richmond was a boomtown!

In droves, men and women arrived in Richmond to work at the Home Front shipyards and factories. They arrived from the urban centers of the East. They came from the poor, rural areas of the South. Via trains, the African-American Pullman porters had spread the word across the country about the relative freedoms and prosperity in California.

From a population of 23,000, Richmond jumped to 100,000 residents within a couple of years. Mostly hungry for jobs—black, brown, white, Mexican, Asian, Native American—they traveled by bus, car, and train. They came however they could. Thousands found free passage on "Henry Kaiser's Magic Carpet" westbound trains. It was wartime. Hundreds of thousands of desperately needed workers came to California to build, build, build!

"In a boomtown, there aren't enough beds," Misty Horn explained. "There aren't enough houses, hotels, trailers, sheds, shacks, chicken coops, apartments, greenhouses, garages, and barns for people to live. That's why some had to sleep in movie theaters. The theaters stayed open twenty-four hours, seven days a week. If you worked days, you slept at night. If you worked nights, you slept during the day. It was the same at the hotels. Beds were used for different people, day and night. They were called 'hot' beds because there was no time to change the sheets. For bathrooms, folks used the sinks and toilets at the train depot and bus station. Believe me, there was always a long, long line."

Around them, the air sizzled with excitement. People were happy to be out. People were happy to have jobs in the war industries. People were happy to be making boomtown wages of one dollar per hour. Crowds strolled through downtown Richmond as if it were a grand carnival.

Missing, however, from the carnival atmosphere were lights. There were no streetlights or neon signs or lights in any windows. All the glass was darkened with black-out curtains. Even the lights on the bridges were blackened on one side. In case of an air attack at night, it would be difficult for enemy planes to find important strategic targets.

"This is different," Mario smiled as he watched the soldiers and sailors in uniform.

"Way different," Maisha said, surveying the men and women in work clothes with their toolboxes and hard hats in their hands.

Blocks of downtown Richmond were lined with a dozen movie theaters, five-and-dime stores, such as Woolworth's, department stores, like J.C. Penney, and restaurants, diners, pharmacies, and hotels. Misty Horn was correct: it was spring 1942.

"Shall we eat?" he asked, patting the roll of dollars in his pocket.

"Pancakes!" Mario and Maisha exclaimed in unison.

"In a boomtown, breakfast is served all day, everyday." Misty Horn observed, guiding them down the street.

"Wop kid, get out!" an inebriated soldier pointed his finger at Mario and cursed.

"Wop?" Mario was bewildered. It seemed as if he was always being mistaken for someone else.

"Kill wops!" the soldier bellowed.

"That's the *N*-word for Italian," Misty Horn translated. "Now, get back," he commanded the soldier. "Or I shall call the MPs."

"You colored folks can get the heck out, too," the soldier retorted as he reeled away.

"Don't worry." Misty Horn gave Mario an affectionate pat. But, Mario was worried. It was not much of a welcome to 1942.

"And blacks?" Maisha asked. "Are we in danger?"

"Before the war, only a few hundred Negroes or colored people, as they were commonly called, lived in Richmond. Nobody thought much about them. There was discrimination in housing and jobs, but the folks were mostly ignored. Then, when thousands came up from the South to work, the prejudice exploded along with the population. Even some well-established blacks did not want Southern Negroes busting into town with their big ideas about freedom, their soul food, and their down-South drawl."

At that moment, Maisha glanced at a sign in a shop window:

NO NEGROES, NO MEXICANS, NO DOGS!

"I'm ashamed to say, these times were not perfect," Misty Horn nodded. "Even if a store let you buy their goods, they did not let blacks try on hats and clothes."

Maisha and Mario understood prejudice. They understood that certain kids had privileges, and they did not. Whether it was color or class, they were unsure.

"I guess we're in for it," Maisha sighed.

"Nobody's going to mess with ya'll this time around," Misty Horn promised.

At Pete's Fountain and Grill on Fifth Street, the windows were covered with dark curtains. However, once inside, the lights blazed. The spiffy chrome counter, the swivel stools, and the leatherette booths were packed with hungry patrons. There was a buzz of conversations and the electric whir of milkshake and malt machines.

Wearing a white starched uniform and a white starched crown, the waitress stared at the odd trio. First, she studied Mario. Next, she scrutinized Maisha and Misty Horn. Then, her eyes roamed back to Mario.

"I can't serve you," she said.

Misty Horn cocked his ear as if he were deaf. "What's that?"

"I'll make an exception and serve you two coloreds. But, I have to turn away the I-ti. He's an enemy alien."

"He's not I-ti or alien or enemy," Maisha said huffily. "He's Mexican."

The waitress asked, "Like the *braceros* that come up here from Mexico?" Thousands of Mexican workers had recently arrived in California to help on the farms and in the factories.

The waitress continued a close inspection of Mario's face. "He don't look Mexican. He looks I-ti."

Maisha blurted angrily, "He's a regular American who lives in Richmond."

"It doesn't matter," Mario said. "I wouldn't eat a pancake at Pete's if it were the last place on earth!"

"He's not I-ti or alien or enemy," Maisha said huffily.

The Wisdom Tree

"Don't let those kind of people get you down," Misty Horn cautioned.

Mario burned with anger. "I hate prejudice."

"Prejudice is something to hate," Misty Horn agreed. "But we're not here long."

"We'll be back in our own Richmond," Maisha reminded them, "with our own prejudices."

"You're right," Misty Horn said. "But as someone who has lived to see the day, I can testify that blacks, Latinos, Asians, women as well as our white brothers and sisters, have taken a few giant steps. We made Barack Hussein Obama the President."

"I guess you have to stand up for everybody," Maisha mused, thinking of the Islamic girls at her school. They were always being teased and taunted for wearing head scarves. Sometimes, they were called "terrorists."

"I go along with Dr. King who said: *Injustice anywhere is a threat to justice everywhere.*"

"That's deep," Mario concluded.

"If you go deep enough, you usually find the truth."

They strolled along Macdonald Avenue among the crowds of people. At the Winters Building, Mario and Maisha were startled by a sign:

 **AIR RAID SHELTER**

"Were there air attacks here in 1942?" Mario asked.

"There were practice drills, alarms, and air-raid sirens. We certainly knew what to do and where to go. Fortunately, we were never bombed."

Across the street, Maisha pointed out a tall, majestic tree. It was so tall that its branches looked as if they grazed the violet clouds. "I recognize that tree," she said.

"It's a fine specimen of Cedar of Lebanon," Misty Horn said. "Back in the day, we called it the 'Wisdom Tree.' We liked to say, 'Meet me at the Wisdom Tree.'"

"Now, it's hidden behind an ugly shopping center," Maisha complained.

Around the Wisdom Tree were other varieties of tall and broad trees that formed the grounds of the Veterans

Memorial Building. There was also a little bandstand. Music drifted into the evening air. Couples danced on a raised wooden platform.

"This is where I met your great-grandmother, Theresa Lyle," Misty Horn reminisced. "I met her the week she came up from Lafayette with her brothers. I had just arrived from Louisiana, too. We were all *greenhorns,* as they liked to say."

Maisha smiled to herself. She was glad that Misty Horn knew Auntie Yates when she was young.

"I knew your great-grandpa, too," he added.

"I wish I had," she said regretfully. "He died a long, long time before I was born."

They stood beside the bandstand, watching couples swing each other over their backs and through their legs in a crazy jitterbug.

A vivacious woman dashed over to Maisha. She cried and threw her arms around the girl's neck. "You must be Theresa Lyle's baby sister!"

"No, ma'm," Maisha said.

"I didn't know Theresa had a sister. A minute ago, Theresa was standing under the Wisdom Tree. Now, I don't see her anywhere."

From the bandstand, a clarinet, an acoustic bass, and

a singer started a jazzy version of "Three Little Fishies," a hit song in 1939. Their new friend sang along:

Down in the meadow in a little bitty pool
Swam three little fishies and a mama fishie, too.
"Swim," said the mama fishie, "Swim if you can."
And they swam and they swam all over the dam.
Boop boop dit-tem dat-tem what-tem Chu!
Boop boop dit-tem dat-tem what-tem Chu!
Boop boop dit-tem dat-tem what-tem Chu!
And they swam and they swam all over the dam.

"Isn't that fun?" she clapped. "Theresa and I love that song. Theresa, where are you?"

"That's okay," Maisha said. "I'm not her sister."

"Ya'll must be kin," the woman argued.

"I'm an only child," Maisha explained.

"Ya'll have to be related somewhere on the family tree. I should know because we spend almost everyday together. We take the train across the Bay Bridge together. We go to welding school together. And guess what?"

Maisha shook her head. She had no idea.

"We plan to be among the first Negro women welders at the Kaiser shipyards. We're going to break the color line and the gender barrier. Our friend, Frances Albrier, is leading the way."

"Right on, sister!" Misty Horn interjected.

The woman held out her delicate hands. "They need small fingers on those ships to weld and rivet in tiny places. We women will build the ships that win the war. You watch!"

The lively lady continued to hum and tap her foot. She smiled and waved at everyone.

"We have to get going," Misty Horn announced. "We're in transit, so to speak."

"Don't be in such a hurry, pops. I want ya'll to meet Theresa."

"We're hungry, right kids?" Misty Horn said hurriedly. A meeting with a close relative was not in the plan.

"Hold up! Let me properly introduce myself so I can join ya'll for dinner. I'm Etta Jefferson. I came from Georgia in 1941 when Kaiser was building the first Liberty ships to help the Brits. I never regretted it a moment. Isn't Richmond the most fun place?" she asked, pinching Maisha's cheeks. "You may not be Theresa's sister, but you are adorable. And you, too," she added, pinching Mario's cheeks.

Mario blushed. He didn't like to be the center of female attention.

"Hey, pops, are you their guardian?" Etta asked Misty Horn.

"That's a good name for it," he replied.

Clubbing in North Richmond

"I bet she took off with Tommy Lee Yates and didn't tell me."

Maisha's heart skipped a beat.

Etta asked, "Have ya'll heard Tommy Lee Yates play and sing? He plays guitar like nobody else. Ya'll hear what I'm saying? He plays the kind of blues that tell you how strong you are. They love him at Tappers' Inn and the Savoy Club. They love him at Dew Drop Inn, the Pink Kitchen, and Brown Derby, too."

"Where's all that?" Mario asked.

"North Richmond," Etta Jefferson said proudly.

Maisha's eyebrows scrunched together. "You mean, North Richmond?"

"Times change, in case you haven't noticed," Misty Horn laughed. "North Richmond is exactly where we're heading. I am salivating for ribs, black-eyed peas, corn-bread, and biscuits with molasses. I figure we'll get good service over there."

"The best!" Etta exclaimed. "But don't get your hopes too high. With rations so strict, sometimes they can't get coffee or meat or sugar or what all. I miss butter and my nylon stockings."

"You can't buy butter?" Mario asked. "Or sugar?"

"Where ya'll kids been? There's a war on, and we can't buy lots of things unless we got a ration card. Even then, we only get so much which really means so little."

Etta applied her red lipstick and straightened the stocking seams along the backs of her calves. "Come on, pops," she said. "I'll give ya'll a ride."

Misty Horn slipped into the passenger seat of a spit-shined 1940 green Chevrolet coupe. Maisha and Mario climbed into the plush back. It was different than Mr. Duggle's Lizzie. Etta didn't have to crank it to start. Nevertheless, it was a rocky ride.

"Are you sure you know how to drive?" Misty Horn asked as they bounced along.

"I grew up driving a tractor," Etta boasted.

"I can tell," Misty Horn muttered under his breath. "Seat belts in cars won't be installed for another twenty-five years. We can thank Ralph Nader for the seat belts that have saved thousands of lives."

Etta flew down Filbert Street and screeched to a stop in front of Tappers' Inn, 715 Chesley Street, North Richmond. Tappers' was a long, low building, set behind a parking lot and its own twenty-four hour gasoline station.

The centerpiece of Tappers' Inn was its elegant bar, backed by mirrors and crowded with elegant, high-styled African-American women and men. It was the most popular club in North Richmond and attracted patrons from all around the Bay.

Call them Negro, colored, African-American, or black, Tappers' Inn was obviously *their* place. Tables with white linen and red leather booths flanked the perimeter of the large dance floor. Not only was there food, drink, music, and dancing, but in the back rooms were slot machines, card games, and a 24-hour barber shop and beauty salon.

They slipped into a booth while Etta went in search of her friends, Theresa and Tommy Lee.

"Tommy Lee! Tommy Lee!" she cried, accosting him in the hall. "You won't believe it!"

"Believe what?" he asked in a Southern drawl. Like Etta, he had come from Georgia, seeking opportunity in California's new war industries.

Etta gazed at Tommy Lee's soft brown eyes, his pencil mustache, and his dimpled smile. If he weren't so stuck on Theresa, she would have claimed him as her boyfriend.

"I met a child who looks like Theresa's lost sister. I want them to meet, but I can't find her anywhere. I bet you know where she is."

"Theresa didn't feel well," Tommy Lee said cooly. "I drove her home."

"These two have got to lay eyes on each other," Etta whined.

"It'll have to wait until tomorrow," he suggested. "Tonight, Theresa has a headache."

"You come with me so I have a witness," Etta insisted.

"Sorry, Etta," Tommy Lee said, removing his electric, hollow-body Gibson guitar from his shoulder and tuning a couple of strings. "I have to run over to the Savoy for my show."

Etta grabbed the guitar strap and tugged. "It won't take you a minute," she said flirtatiously. "I know you already tuned that old thing about a hundred times tonight."

The gentle smile vanished from Tommy Lee's face.

"Miss Jefferson," he commanded, "remove your paw from my guitar."

"Paw?" Etta jerked her hand away.

Without another word, Tommy Lee wheeled around. He headed out the back door towards the Savoy.

An irate Etta Jefferson returned to the dining room.

It was filled with the bustle of waiters and patrons, eaters and drinkers. Large platters of food were delivered. Stacks of empty plates and glasses were bussed away. The band musicians tuned their instruments and chatted with patrons as they got ready to play.

"I certainly hope Theresa Lyle doesn't plan to marry Tommy Lee Yates," Etta fumed.

"She'll marry him," Maisha asserted.

Etta turned a sharp eye on the girl. "What makes you so sure?" she snapped. "You're not her sister. You claim ya'll never met. But you're going on like an authority on her future."

Misty Horn interrupted, "Miss Jefferson, you know how youngsters wag their tongue. Please, don't take it seriously."

"Tommy Lee Yates is not a man you can trust," Etta whimpered. "He may look like a gentleman, but it's a costume he puts on and takes off. It's a stage act like everything else he does."

"We thought you really liked him," Mario said.

Etta blushed. "I once liked him, but I do not like him now." Her mood had turned sour. Her excitement had drained away. "I'll drive you back downtown. I know I'm ready to leave."

"We'll get around on our own," Misty Horn replied. "We want to roam through North Richmond and take in the sights."

"Thank you for the ride, Miss Jefferson," Mario and Maisha said.

"Yes, thank you," Misty Horn echoed.

"I guess I won't mention anything to Theresa since you're not related," she said.

"That's fine," Maisha nodded, winking at Misty Horn. "Maybe, we'll meet in another lifetime."

The Blues

A few blocks from Tappers' Inn, the Savoy Club on Chesley Street offered an entirely different atmosphere. Instead of white linen, checkered oilcloth was slapped on wooden tables. Instead of mirrors and multi-color lights, the Savoy was as plain and funky as a roadhouse in rural Mississippi. However, like Tappers', the Savoy served some of the best classic Southern cuisine—ribs, fried chicken, and greens—courtesy of Willie Mae "Granny" Johnson, the owner.

Misty Horn and the two youngsters squeezed into the back of a crowded, smoky room. A hundred people sat or stood, waiting for the show to begin. It was Granny Johnson, dressed in a blue sequin dress, who entered the stage, greeted by round of loud, raucous applause.

"Ladies and gentlemen, welcome to North Richmond and the Savoy!" Granny Johnson waved. "I know you didn't come to hear me play tonight!"

There was a ripple of laughter. A man shouted, "You got that right!"

Granny Johnson smiled into the spotlights. Behind her, the house band sat with their instruments, waiting for her routine to end. Finally, she announced:

"Without further ado, let me introduce the great Tommy Lee Yates!"

Maisha swooned with pride as the applause thundered all around her.

A slender, light-skinned brown man with a gray fedora and a loose gray tie strolled onto the stage and into the halo of a single spotlight. At first, he didn't look at the audience or the band. He didn't speak. He didn't strum the strings of his guitar. He simply sat on a stool, waiting for the audience to settle into their places, remove their coats, and lean back in their chairs.

Then, he started to play: one chord, two chords, ten chords spun quickly through the air. It didn't seem possible that human fingers could work so quickly. Tommy Lee molded and bent the sound as if he were teasing, fighting, and loving the story inside the notes. When the band joined in, the room exploded.

Waves of emotion filled Maisha. For her, Tommy Lee Yates had been a remote and shadowy figure. Occasionally, Auntie Yates mentioned him. Occasionally, Auntie Yates said, "Tommy Lee would love that."

However, Tommy Lee was long dead. Although it was a sad fact, Maisha never paid it much attention.

After a couple of songs, Tommy Lee started to sing. As soon as he opened his mouth, several women began to wail.

They shouted his name, "Tommy Lee! Tommy Lee!"

They yelled, "Tell it, brother."

They called, "Play your song."

Tommy Lee displayed no reaction. It appeared that he was wandering inside the music, faraway from the Savoy and North Richmond. When the song ended, applause filled the room to the rafters.

Tommy Lee bowed his head to the audience and nodded to the other musicians. After a few more numbers, he mopped his face with a handkerchief and stood up.

"We'll take a short break, folks," he said to the crowd.

Still, the applause did not stop. The crowd insisted that Tommy Lee return for one more song. Just as he began, he leaned into the microphone and whispered, "I'd like to dedicate this to my girl, Theresa Lyle. Let's hope she's feeling a little better."

Maisha grabbed Mario's hand. "He's talking about Auntie Yates."

"I know," Mario said. He was excited, too. He had those same kind of feelings whenever he visited his *abuelita* in Mexico. He knew how it felt to belong to a place, a culture, and a people. He was happy for Maisha.

It appeared that he was wandering inside the music, faraway from the Savoy and North Richmond.

To the Future

When Tommy Lee and the band stopped playing, it was dawn. Instead of the usual two shows, he played three. Late, late into the night and wee hours of morning, he played with musicians who stopped by to jam.

Granny Johnson paid little attention to Maisha and Mario. She fed them a midnight supper and let them stay all night at the club.

"Once in a lifetime," Misty Horn proclaimed after the last encore.

While the musicians packed up their instruments, Maisha looked wistfully towards the stage. She wasn't sure that she wanted to meet Tommy Lee Yates. She wasn't sure what she would do or say.

"Don't speak to him," Misty Horn warned. "We were lucky to avoid meeting Auntie Yates. If you exchange words, you risk permanent residency in the past."

"Permanent residency in the past?" Maisha repeated slowly.

"You break the chronology of your own blood. It's different with Etta Jefferson or Mr. Duggle or our Ohlone girl. They're like many people in any life. They come and go. They ebb and flow. But your great-grandfather is your ancestor. If you speak to him, there's a chance you won't get back to your own time."

"You mean the time we were born?" Mario asked.

"Yes, everyone is born into their own time and no other. We stepped out of our own time for a few hours, but you have your own lives waiting."

"Will you get his autograph?" Maisha cried.

"Let me try," Misty Horn said.

From the back of the club, Maisha and Mario watched as Misty Horn shuffled across the Savoy's floor. Granny Johnson's helpers were hard at work, sweeping and mopping up the cornbread crumbs, the splashes of beer, and the butts of cigarettes and cigars.

"What if Misty Horn gets caught in a permanent residency in the past?" Mario asked.

"That's a frightening thought," Maisha said.

"We should have asked him for Plan B," Mario added nervously.

"Look! He's speaking to Tommy Lee Yates!" Tommy Lee slapped Misty Horn on the back as if he knew him.

"He couldn't know him," Mario said.

"Well, he once knew him," Maisha reminded him.

"That was over sixty years ago when Misty Horn looked a whole lot different."

"He's a strange man, isn't he?" Maisha mused. "He's someone outside his own time *and* at home in any time."

They watched as Misty Horn held out a matchbook. Whatever he said made Tommy Lee laugh and slap his back again. Tommy Lee reached for the matchbook. Before he wrote on the inside flap, he looked far across the room at Maisha. For a split second, their eyes locked. Then, he scribbled a few words and his signature.

When Misty Horn returned with the precious matchbook, Maisha was trembling. She opened the flap and read:

To your bright future,

Tommy Lee Yates, Blues Man

The Shipyards

Early morning light glowed over North Richmond. The air and earth smelled fresh and sweet. From Third Street to Market, there were vegetables growing in every yard. Empty lots and fields were planted with fruit trees and vegetables, too.

"Victory gardens," Misty Horn said. "Everyone in America has a little victory garden. Even in the cities people are growing vegetables. It's part of the war effort."

"A good peace effort, too," Mario commented.

"You can make that happen when you're the President," Misty Horn winked.

"I want to be a doctor," Mario said.

"All the better. Healers and doctors are the great peacemakers."

A bus with "SHIPYARDS" displayed on its window pulled up to the corner. "That's us," Misty Horn announced. "Our last stop before home."

The bus was crowded with workers in work clothes, wearing photo badges and carrying metal lunch pails. Most of them were headed to the Kaiser shipyards. However, there were fifty other war-related factories in Richmond. The Ford Motor Company Assembly Plant converted automobiles to tanks and jeeps. American Standard changed bathtubs into hand grenades.

Buses ran around Richmond morning, noon, and night. In addition, Kaiser workers used a sixteen-mile "Shipyard Railway" to travel between 40th Street in Oakland and the Richmond yards. This railway was created from discarded New York city train cars that had been shipped around Cape Horn to the Bay Area. There was also the Key Route system of streetcars, trains, and ferries between the East Bay and San Francisco. Trains traveled back and forth on the lower deck of the Bay Bridge. Workers, who did not use public transportation, were encouraged to carpool, not only to save gasoline for the war, but more importantly, to conserve rubber.

The bus stopped at Kaiser Yard No. 3 just as an eight-hour work shift changed. A mob of exhausted workers checked out while a mob of fresh workers checked in. The shipyards operated around the clock.

"That's hecka people!" Maisha exclaimed.

Indeed, it was a human sea of thousands of men and women of all colors and all backgrounds. Among them were African-Americans, mostly from the South, Mexican-Americans, Chinese, Native Americans, and many poor white farmers or Okies from the dry, rural belt of the country called the Dust Bowl.

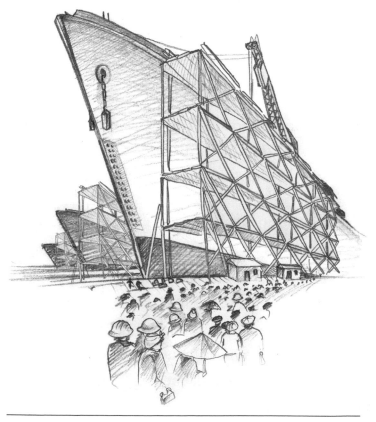

Indeed, it was a human sea of thousands of men and women of all colors and all backgrounds.

"Cool!" Mario stood in amazement as he focused on the intricate scaffolding that surrounded an enormous steel ship. "That's the biggest thing I've ever seen!"

The shipyard was a beehive of activity. Inside the pre-assembly plant, metal pieces were perfectly measured and cut. Then, giant whirley cranes took over. Supported by four huge pillars that rolled on tracks, the cranes moved the heavy metal pieces to the waterfront where welders, riveters, fitters, burners, and electricians assembled them into seaworthy vessels.

Not only was the shipyard full of activity, but it was also a volcano of noise. The machines, the hammering, the signal and ship whistles, the loudspeakers, the trains, and the shouting of directions could be heard a mile away.

During World War II, no other place in America built as many ships as the four Kaiser shipyards on the Richmond waterfront. Over 740 ships in four years were launched. Richmond Kaiser held the record for the quickest ship built: the *Robert E. Peary* took four days, fifteen hours, and twenty-nine minutes!

"I wish we could view a launching," Misty Horn sighed. "What a party! After a bottle of fine champagne is cracked over the ship's bow, there are stirring speeches by movie stars and dignitaries, followed by musical entertainment. No one enjoys a launch as much as the workers who built the ship."

"I guess they won't let us past the gate," Mario said with disappointment.

"Absolutely not," Misty Horn confirmed. "Shipyards are top security sites. No one goes in or out without a badge. In addition, people got badly hurt, working on these ships. It was dangerous. They got burned from welding. They got fevers, chills, and nausea from zinc fumes. They broke bones. Boilers blew up. Heavy things fell and crushed them. Almost as many died in industrial accidents on the Home Front as in combat."

As if in response, two ambulances raced into the shipyard and loaded up stretchers with workers.

"They're off to The Field Hospital on Cutting Boulevard," Misty Horn said. "Twenty-four hour shuttles carry injured workers to the First Aid stations. If they're seriously injured or sick, they go to The Field Hospital or Kaiser Hospital in Oakland. Every shipyard worker has health insurance. Dr. Garfield and the other Kaiser doctors take good care of them."

"Who looked after the kids if everyone worked all crazy hours?" Maisha asked.

"Yes, the kids!" Misty Horn twirled his fingers in the air. "Since the war industries needed women to work, Kaiser and others set up twenty-four hour centers to take care of the babies and tots. As for schools, the kids went in half-day shifts since the classrooms were so crowded. They also brought in portables to take care of the overflow. The schools were in double sessions, and Stege had four sessions per day."

"And when the war ended?" Mario wondered.

"Most shipyards and daycare centers shut down. Period. No advance warning, no severance pay. They closed. People had come to California, looking for the American dream, but once the boom economy of the war was over, it was hard. There were not enough jobs. After the men returned from war, the strong, independent women were expected to go home. Suddenly, employers rejected the idea of women doing men's work. They fired the women and people of color, too."

"That's cold!" Maisha cried indignantly.

"Times change," Misty Horn smiled inscrutably. "In case you haven't noticed."

Away to the Present

A ruddy-faced man in uniform tapped Mario on the back with a nightstick.

"Ow-ow!" Mario wheeled around.

"How come you kids ain't in school?" the truant officer asked.

"They're visiting from elsewhere, sir," Misty Horn quickly explained. "I wanted to show them the Kaiser shipyards."

"Visiting from where?"

"From Richmond," Maisha blurted.

"She means Richmond, Virginia," Misty Horn interjected.

"And Michoacan, Mexico," Mario spoke up.

The officer removed his cap and scratched his head. He scratched long and hard. "Ain't I seen you two downtown, making trouble? You sure are dressed like troublemakers."

"No, officer," Misty Horn was polite but firm. "The clothes are homemade like all kids wear today. Their mother doesn't know how to sew. That's why they look so funny."

Again, the policeman scratched his head. Flakes of dandruff rained on his dark uniform. "One comes from Virginia and the other from Mexico? And you say they have the same mother? That don't make sense."

"Look closely," Misty Horn suggested.

The truant officer peered into Maisha's and Mario's faces. "I guess they favor each other, but the girl, she's colored."

Mario and Maisha smiled nervously.

The man replaced his cap and brushed his shoulders. "With every mother working in the shipyards, we get nothing but trouble from kids. You two ain't been stealing tires?"

"We're not stealing anything," Mario said.

"Stealing rubber is a serious offense," the officer frowned. "I got to take your names in case you get in trouble again."

"We haven't been in trouble once," Maisha protested.

"You talking back to a policeman?" the man glared.

"No, sir," she said.

"So, what's your name?"

"Maisha Yates," she replied.

"Y - A - T - E - S? Any kin to Tommy Lee Yates?" he asked.

Maisha beamed with pride. Maybe, the truant officer was a blues fan. Maybe, he wanted to check out Maisha's autograph. She touched the matchbook in the pocket of her hoodie.

"That colored boy comes into our city and thinks he can rule the world. He is one uppity negra."

"You mean, African-American," Misty Horn corrected.

"African what?" the truant officer roared. "I guess we will take a little trip downtown."

Mario looked at Misty Horn, begging him to do something. And quick! Unfortunately, Misty Horn was tired. He was old and tired. His powers were worn down. Nevertheless, he took Maisha and Mario by the hand and closed his eyes.

A breeze began to blow. It blew stronger and stronger. It whipped the bay waters along the sides of the ships. It whipped the flags on the flagpoles. A loud whistle blew in the shipyards. It was a high-wind advisory for workers to come down quickly from dangerous and precarious places.

The sound of the wind was familiar to Maisha and Mario. They tightly shut their eyes. They held onto Misty Horn. They braced themselves against a wind so fierce that it almost blew them over.

When the wind subsided, they opened their eyes. They were on Macdonald Avenue. The day was cold, dank, and gray. The wet leaves shimmered. Large, heavy raindrops dropped from the trees. The #72 bus rumbled by. With great relief and some disappointment, Maisha and Mario were back in their Richmond. They had returned to their own time.

A few blocks away, the sound of gunshots faded. A late-model car squealed away. Almost instantly, police cars converged on the scene. An ambulance from Kaiser Permanente Hospital careened around the corner.

The sirens and shouts filled Maisha with sadness. So much of Richmond had been lost: the wild abundance of the Ohlone world; the optimism of the early twentieth century; the energy and hope of workers fighting a war from the Home Front.

The EMT lifted a limp body from the sidewalk. They placed it in the back of the ambulance. Maisha couldn't tell if the victim were alive or not. However, she knew it could have been Mario, her mother, or herself caught in the crossfire.

"Mario," she said tenderly, "we're different now."

"I know," he replied tenderly in return.

She touched his mangled ear. "What will you tell your *madre?*"

"I'll tell her I fell," Mario said.

"You did fall," Maisha reassured him. "You fell into the hands of the wrong people at the wrong time. It wasn't your time. It was theirs."

"It's not a lie when you put it like that," Mario said. "What will you say about your cheek?"

"I guess I'll say I fell, too."

Celebration and Mourning

On Saturday afternoon, the Laundromat-*Lavanderia* was filled with Mexican, Laotian, African-American, El Salvadorean, Samoan, Guatemalan, Middle Eastern, and Filipina women. They were a few men, too. Everyone was waiting for the machines to stop, start, empty, and start again. It was a miniature United Nations.

The dryers made the air humid and warm. Suds from the washers sent a clean, fresh smell throughout the large room. Steam clouded the windows that faced Harbour Way.

Linda Yates and Sylvia Reyes stood side by side, folding their clean clothes.

"Have you noticed anything different about Mario recently?" Linda asked.

Sylvia's eyes widened. "*Si, si!*" she said. "Since their visit with Misty Horn, Mario sees that the world is bigger than himself. It's as if his mind has expanded. What about Maisha?"

"It's the same," Linda enthused. "She has confidence that she'll fulfill her biggest dreams."

"Tell me about Misty Horn."

"I don't know him well," Linda said in a low voice. "I met him when I married Simon. Like Simon's family, he also came to Richmond from Louisiana during World War II. He likes to blab about other worlds and other dimensions. Usually, I tune out. You see, I'm a down-to-earth person. I have enough trouble making sense of this world," Linda laughed. "However, I will never say another cold word about Misty Horn. He has had a positive influence on my Maisha."

"I want to invite him for Christmas," Sylvia said. "Will you all come, too?"

Linda hugged her friend. "*Gracias*, Sylvia. It's our first holiday without Simon. Your large family will make it easier for us."

Sylvia piled the fresh towels and sheets into two large baskets. Linda folded the shirts that she had bought to mail to Simon in Texas.

"We'll bring our cornbread, glazed ham, Auntie Yates' crab cakes, and pecan pies," she said.

Sylvia bubbled with excitement. "Don't bring too much because our *abuelita* will import the entire meal with her from Mexico. Let's hope they let her on the airplane with her rebozo and bags of shredded coconut candy, sweet potato jam, salty cheese, and *adobo*. After you eat *abuelita's* Christmas dinner, I promise you won't move for two days."

The washing, drying, and folding were nearly done. The two women packed up their boxes of soap and jugs of bleach.

"Tomorrow, we pick up our *abuelita* from the airport," Sylvia said. "We're so happy. It's her first trip on a plane."

"Tomorrow is Shannon Cooper's funeral," Linda Yates reported sadly.

"Was he the boy killed last week?"

"He died in his brother's arms," Linda muttered softly. "Maisha is heartbroken."

"Oh, I'm so sorry. Were they good friends?" Sylvia asked.

"They were the absolute opposite of friends. Shannon and Sammy Cooper were cruel to her. Here in Richmond, we've lost so many. It's hard on all the kids. Maisha says that Shannon died without knowing his future or his past."

Sylvia Reyes shuddered with sorrow. "If we can go

to the moon, surely we can make a safe world for our children."

"Tomorrow, we'll be mourning Shannon Cooper. We'll be mourning whoever shot him. We'll be mourning our community."

The two women draped their arms around each other. They knew exactly what the other one was thinking. Their eyes filled with tears and their hearts filled with hope for Richmond's children.

Linda whispered, "May they all find a beautiful future."

The Holiday Feast

Inside the Reyes' apartment, a festive table was laid out with many dishes of food. As Sylvia predicted, their *abuelita* transported bags of treats from Mexico. She also spent her first days in Upper California, presiding over the Reyes' stove. Auntie Yates and Linda brought their favorite holiday dishes. Maisha made sugar cookies baked in the shape of angels and stars.

The centerpiece of the table was a plate of oranges and a small tree with tinsel. Under the tree were wrapped gifts, one for each person, bought at the Dollar Store. Everyone loved the game of picking out a surprise present.

Two special gifts, however, did not go under the tree. One was a polished abalone shell that Mario gave to his *abuelita*.

"*Que bello!*" Señora Guardado exclaimed.

The other was a string of cowry shells that Maisha gave to Auntie Yates.

"They don't look as if they came from this world!" she marveled.

Misty Horn winked. "Of this world, but not of this time," he said mysteriously.

"Did Seeker give you these things?" Linda teased.

"You might say that," Misty Horn replied.

Throughout the party, Keeper and her new friend, Señora Guardado, sat beside each other on the couch, knitting and speaking softly in a combination of Spanish and English. The two women understood each other perfectly. Both had worked since they were children. Both knew poverty, struggle, hard times, better times, and the rewards of work. They had much in common.

Auntie Yates had been raised in rural Louisiana in a time when blacks had no rights. They certainly could not vote or serve on juries or be elected to public office. Most could not own property. Most were sharecroppers with huge debts to white Southern landowners. Their children went to poor, segregated schools. Few were able to attend college.

Señora Guardado had been born on a large agave plantation in Michoacan where peons were treated almost like slaves. Only a few years of school were available to their children. Like the black sharecroppers, the poor farmers were tied to the rich *patrones* in an endless cycle of debt. It was almost impossible to escape.

"It seems as if they have been best friends for a hundred years," Linda observed.

Sylvia took Linda's hand. "Everyone is glad to be together. What better gift?"

Auntie Yates and Señora Guardado leaned into each other's ears. Their knitting needles clicked as the colored yarn spun into baby blankets and baby booties. They looked like two contented old women, happy to sit and knit.

However, they were deep into a discussion of the environment. Señora Guardado was one of Michoacan's leading champions of clean water rights. She constantly spoke out. She constantly wrote letters and organized protests. Because of her work, her life had been threatened. Once, her house had been burned.

Auntie Yates was a community organizer for clean air in Richmond. She had gone up against the city government. She had gone up against the oil and chemical companies. She had traveled to Sacramento and Washington to testify before lawmakers.

"The wind blows the bad air to us," Auntie Yates said. "It makes the people *enfermo*. It makes our communities *enfermo*."

"*Si, si*," Señora Guardado understood. "*Los* corporations throw *la química* in our *agua*."

"Things change only when the people change them," the two women both agreed. They had lived through many changes, good and bad. However, their battle for clean air and clean water would soon pass to the younger generation. Likely, they would not live to see the battle won.

"There's a movie starting for the little kids," Sylvia called over to Maisha and Mario. "Do you two want to watch *Bambi*?"

"I've seen it," Maisha said. "I even remember when it came out."

Sylvia checked the date on the DVD. "1942? I don't think so," she smiled indulgently. "You must be thinking of *A Bug's Life*."

"What are those two up to?" Linda asked, watching them huddle on the floor with Misty Horn.

"Top secret, no doubt," Sylvia said.

Mario was grinning, as he pulled on his earlobe. Misty Horn was chuckling, as he yanked Mario's hands behind his back. Maisha sat doubled over with laughter.

"Don't keep bothering your ear," Sylvia reminded him.

"It's healed," Mario said, continuing to pull and laugh.

"What's so funny?" a bewildered Sylvia asked Linda.

"Frankly, I don't think we'll ever know."

New Year's Day

On January first, Misty Horn invited Mario and Maisha to stop by his house. "To give a toast to Janus," he said.

"A friend of yours?" Mario inquired.

"Janus is everyone's friend," Misty Horn winked.

It was a cold, sunny New Year's Day. Mario and Maisha bundled themselves in hats, scarves, and gloves for their visit. Along with a bag of *abuelita's* coconut candy, they brought the last rose of the year from Linda Yates' garden for their friend, Misty Horn.

Richmond's streets were empty. There was no traffic or noise. The biting cold lay like a blanket over the city. The Iron Triangle was quiet, too, not ghostly but calm and serene.

When they arrived, Misty Horn's little fireplace was ablaze. Bowls of hot chocolate and slices of lemon cake awaited them. The three sat together on his velveteen sofa.

"Meet Janus," Misty Horn said, holding up a small bronze head.

"Hola! Janus!" Mario shouted.

Maisha stared at the identical bearded faces on either side of Janus' head. One face looked to the left. The other looked to the right. Janus reminded Maisha of Sammy and Shannon Cooper: two faces, nearly the same, one alive and one dead. During the past weeks, almost everything called to mind the Cooper brothers.

Carefully, Mario examined the bronze head. "I already met this guy in Nevin Park."

Misty Horn smiled at the boy's sense of humor. Mario had a knack for finding the funny side in almost everything.

"In Roman mythology, Janus was the god of doors and gates, beginnings and endings. Janus looked forward and back, out and in, past and future."

"Is that why we call the first month of the year, January?" Maisha asked.

"Exactly," Misty Horn confirmed. "The names of months and days have their roots in Greek numbers and Roman gods. Today, we use the Gregorian calendar, but time is complicated."

Mario and Maisha exchanged a look of perfect understanding. The past was not only in their own time. Now, they shared it with an Ohlone girl, Mr. Duggle, seven Chinese immigrants, the Esteban family, Etta Jefferson, and Tommy Lee Yates.

Misty Horn said, "Every civilization has tried to figure out the measurements of time. In 1752 in America, Wednesday, September 2nd was followed by Thursday, September 14th to make the necessary adjustments."

"That's too crazy!" Mario exclaimed.

"Fortunately, we have Leap Year to tidy up our extra minutes. Calendars from the Egyptians, Aztecs, Babylonians, and Mayans are also interesting," Misty Horn droned on.

However, Mario and Maisha had stopped listening. They were nodding sleepily in time with the old man's murmuring voice.

"Ready for your New Year's gift?" Misty Horn asked, clapping loudly.

Maisha and Mario sat up with a start.

"That's cold," Maisha said.

"We were in dreamland," Mario added.

"Time to wake up! Your gift is waiting upstairs, or rather, *outstairs*."

Mario's eyebrows rose. Maisha's brow wrinkled.

"But we're so warm and comfortable *instairs*," they protested.

"Yes, *in* is comfortable, but we're going *out*."

The Last Egg

"I'd like to stay right here today," Maisha said, stepping back.

Misty Horn stood by the last egg on the shelf. "I thought we might make one more tiny trip," he winked.

Maisha and Mario gave each other a questioning look. "Is that our New Year's gift?" Mario asked.

"It will be brief," Misty Horn promised.

The threesome peered into the last egg where they read a banner: **2050.**

"The future!" Mario whispered excitedly.

"Now stare," Misty Horn commanded. "Stare until your eyeballs ache. Stare until your eyes can't stay open a second longer."

Outside, tree limbs rocked. The wind gusted. Showers of papery leaves fell from branches. Windows and doors rattled. They stared until they had to close their eyes.

When they opened them, Misty Horn nodded towards the passing parade of dancers, musicians, and horse-drawn hay wagons carrying children. "A Garden Festival, if I'm not mistaken."

Mario and Maisha blinked. Perhaps, it was Macdonald Avenue, or not. The thoroughfare for motor vehicles had drastically shrunk. Instead, there was a wide, spotless path crowded with skaters, pedestrians, baby strollers, bicyclists, and folks in wheelchairs. A long, sleek electric train ran silently down the median with a destination sign: FERRY POINT.

"Trains heading to Ferry Point have a familiar ring," Mario grimaced.

"It took a while for the trains and ferries to come back. Most of the best ideas have been discovered, then forgotten, and then found again. As in 1915, lots of ferries crisscross the Bay in 2050. There are so few cars that much of the land has been reclaimed. The asphalt roads, the concrete sidewalks, the highways, the gas stations, and car lots are parks for everyone. Look! There's a 'peace' garden," Misty Horn smiled joyfully. "You may recall that was your idea, Mario. Every other city block has a vacant lot dedicated to gardens for fruits and vegetables."

They strolled along, passing garden after garden, hearing chickens, and seeing an occasional cow. All the children and adults greeted them. "Hello, neighbor," they said.

"Hello, neighbor," Misty Horn greeted in return.

Mario and Maisha were too embarrassed to say anything, but eventually, they replied, "Hello, neighbor."

"People seem really happy," Maisha observed.

"They eat healthy food. They work less. They labor at jobs that suit them. They walk and bicycle. They tend to their gardens. They have time to do the things they love," Misty Horn explained. "It's a simple formula."

Richmond's handsome buildings had either been refurbished or rebuilt with interesting, architectural details. Small shops carried handmade clothing, baskets, woven rugs, and other articles. The delicious smell of freshly baked bread drifted through the air. Family-owned restaurants offered food specialities from all over the world. Every window displayed the same sign: *All ingredients are local and organic!*

"What happened to 'fast' food?" Mario asked.

"Times change," Misty Horn said what he always said.

At the corner of Harbour Way, the garden of their childhood had expanded into a large plaza. The Wisdom Tree was now so tall that it was nearly impossible to see its top. Scattered throughout the plaza were tables and chairs where people enjoyed drinks and snacks. Everywhere, the pleasant songs of birds filled the air.

"And the shopping center?" Maisha puzzled.

"It was your generation who made the big changes. You grew up determined to make a better and more beautiful world. You kids went way outside the box." Misty Horn's hands waved in all directions, "This is your Richmond."

Mario and Maisha turned around in amazement. When their eyes caught the name, *The Shannon and Sammy Cooper Institute,* a stunned Maisha asked, "Our Sammy Cooper?"

"Sammy Cooper figured out a way to help Richmond kids in gangs claim a future without guns, violence, and crime. Then, he carried his vision all over the world."

"Our Sammy Cooper?" Maisha repeated in shock.

"People change, too," Misty Horn said.

"What about Mario?" Maisha asked.

"You mean Dr. Mario Reyes? His neighborhood family clinics are used as a model across the country."

Mario said proudly, "I don't know what that means, but I guess I'll find out."

"And me?" Maisha asked shyly.

"Come, let's look at the statue of your Auntie Yates in the plaza. She was a shining light to your generation."

"Our Sammy Cooper?" Maisha repeated in shock.

In the center of Richmond Plaza stood a beautiful life-size ceramic sculpture of Maisha's great-grandmother. Beside it were statues of other women and men, their hands linked and their mouths open as if they were singing. Underneath was a plaque with their names and the contributions they made to save the planet from environmental disaster.

"When Auntie Yates died, she had to pass the torch. Guess who picked it up?"

Maisha's eyes welled with tears. "Me?"

"Remember, how much you admired the baskets of the Ohlone people?" he asked.

Maisha nodded, feeling for the tiny bird-bone whistle that she always wore around her neck.

"From that moment, you understood that beauty is inspired by the beauty around us. If beauty is erased from the world, something dies within us. If beauty surrounds us, we too find inspiration with our hands, our hearts, and our minds. It is the gift we give each other."

"Me?" Maisha was overwhelmed with emotion.

Misty Horn said solemnly, "The future is not written in a book. It is not inscribed in stone. The future is only our hopes and dreams. It's up to you to make them happen."

Spring Again

Simon Yates returned from his job in Texas to his family and friends in Richmond. Everyone was happy to see him, Maisha most of all. After he settled in with his new job, she asked her daddy if they could ride around and look at sights in the city. At the top of her list was Ferry Point, followed by the Richmond Museum of History, the Rosie the Riveter Monument, and the old Ford plant.

"You know more about Richmond than I do," Simon said.

Maisha blushed with pleasure. "The Ford plant made 60,000 tanks during World War II," she reported eagerly. "Whenever they shipped out a tank or jeep, they put a newspaper or magazine inside so the soldiers would have something to read."

"How did you learn so much in such a short time?" her father stammered in awe. "I haven't been gone that long."

"Misty Horn helped us," she said slyly. "He taught us to look closely at the past because sometimes you can see the future."

Simon Yates did a double-take. "Linda," he called out to the kitchen, "did Maisha turn into a genius while I was away?"

Linda laughed. "Have you forgotten how curious our girl is?"

"Curiosity is asking a million questions," Simon said, pulling Maisha onto his lap. "Now, the girl has answers. I bet you found out why it's called the Iron Triangle, too."

Maisha put her arms around her daddy's neck and gave him a ferocious hug. "I found out lots of things."

"It's good for your education for me to leave town," he teased.

"No! No! No!" Maisha held him tightly.

"Now what's the plan for the garden today?" Simon asked, gazing at the bright, blue California sky. Rain was expected in a couple of days, making it perfect weather to plant.

"Mario has the plans," Maisha said. "It'll be beautiful."

Mario arrived with a diagram of the garden. He had used graph paper to divide the backyard into small, separate sections for flowers, vegetables, and a variety of citrus that thrived in Richmond's climate.

"Where did you two get such an idea?" Simon asked.

"We got inspired by the Victory gardens during World War II," Mario explained.

"You kids!" Simon slapped his thigh. "You're going to change the world!"

"That's the idea," Mario and Maisha said in unison.

"Shall we get going?" Simon rubbed his hands together. He loved working in the earth. He loved helping Auntie Yates in her garden. However, he never imagined using the backyard of their apartment house to grow their own food.

"Papá is already in the back with the compost and mulch," Mario said.

"Yasmine and Carolina are coming over to help, too."

"Hola! Manuel!" Simon shouted through the open window. "We'll be down in a minute."

Maisha winked at Mario, "He means *in*, not down."

Mario doubled over with laughter. "Don't even think of mentioning that."

THE END

Reference Materials

Allen, Robert L. *The Port Chicago Mutiny, The Story of the Largest Mass Mutiny Trial in U. S. Naval History*. Berkeley, CA: Heyday Books, 1993.

Bastin, Donald. *Images of America: Richmond*. Charleston, SC, Portsmouth, NH, San Francisco, CA: Arcadia Publishing, 2003.

Birth of Victory, documentary film about the Kaiser shipyards.

Camp, William Martin. *Skip to My Lou*. Garden City, New York: Doubleday, Doran & Company, 1945.

"Cement Curbs, Hotels and Wooden Palace Cars: The Pullman Company in Richmond California" by James A. Herbst. City of Richmond website.

Chall, Malka. Interview with Frances Albrier. Berkeley: Regional Oral History Office, Bancroft Library, University of California, Berkeley.

Dunning, Judith K. Interviews in "On the Waterfront: An Oral History of Richmond, California," with Margaret Louise Cathay, Eddie Eaton, Selena Foster, Dominic Ghio, Joseph Perrelli, Lewis Napoleon Van Hook. Berkeley: Regional Oral History Office, Bancroft Library, University of California, Berkeley.

Evanosky, Dennis and Kos, Eric J. *East Bay Then & Now*, San Diego, CA: Thunder Bay Press, 2004.

Executive Order No. 9066, Authorizing the Secretary of War to Prescribe Military Areas, February 19, 1942.

Exhibits at Richmond Museum of History, Richmond, CA, 2005-2008.

Exhibits at Phoebe A. Hearst Museum of Anthropology, Kroeber Hall, University of California, Berkeley.

Fabry, Joseph. *Swing Shift: Building the Liberty Ships*. San Francisco, CA: Strawberry Hill Press, 1982.

Field, Connie, producer/director. *The Life and Times of Rosie the Riveter*, documentary film, 1980.

Gilford, Steve. Conversation and correspondence regarding the Kaiser shipyards, 2006, 2009.

Gilford, Steve. *On This Date in KP History* #229 & #230 "60 Years Ago: September 26, 1942, Henry Kaiser's Magic Carpet: New York City to Portland, Oregon;" #232 "Celebrating a Medical Center's Anniversary and an Emotional Reunion;" #239 "Permanente Medicine in the Kaiser Shipyards—1942;" #240 "Continuing the Story of Permanente Medicine in the Kaiser Shipyards;" #248 "African-American Liberty Ships and the Kaiser Shipyards;" #307 "Rosie, the Riveter;" #308 "A Search for the 'Real' Rosie the Riveter;" #309 "Looking Further Back in History to See if There Could Be an 'Original' Rosie the Riveter;" #310

"Rosie the Riveter: She Gets a Face;" #311 "Rosie Becomes a Household Name and Steps into History."

Graves, Donna. *Mapping Richmond's World War II Home Front: A Historical Report Prepared for the National Park Service, Rosie the Riveter/World War II Home Front National Historical Park*, 2004.

Hulaniski, F.J., editor. *The History of Contra Costa County, California*. Chapter 26 by Henry Colman Cutting, pp. 326-354. Berkeley, CA: The Elms Publishing Co., Inc., 1917.

Johnson, Marilynn S. *The Second Gold Rush: Oakland and the East Bay in World War II*. Berkeley, CA: University of California Press, 1993.

KCET Online, *California at War*.

LaMarr, Jean and assistants. *The Ohlone Journey*, commentary and mural, Berkeley, CA, 1995.

Leffland, Ella. *Rumors of Peace*. New York: Harper & Row, 1979.

Lemke-Santangel, Gretchen. *Abiding Courage: African American Migrant Women and the East Bay Community*. Chapel Hill, NC: University of North Carolina Press, 1996.

Margolin, Malcolm. *The Ohlone Way*. Berkeley, CA: Heyday Books, 1978.

Moore, Shirley Ann Wilson. *To Place Our Deeds: The African American Community in Richmond, California, 1910-1963*. Berkeley, CA: University of California Press, 1993.

Moore, Shirley Ann Wilson. Lecture on World War II blues clubs and BBQ joints in North Richmond. Richmond Museum of History, Richmond, CA, 2004.

National Park Service, *Rosie the Riveter: WWII Home Front,* Feasibility Study, prepared by the Planning and Partnership Team National Park Service, June 2000.

Prelinger Library, Rick and Megan Shaw Prelinger.

Prescott, Amelie. *The Ohlone Journey,* documentary video, 1995.

"Richmond Took a Beating," Fortune Magazine, February 1945.

Richmond's World War II sites, bus tour sponsored by the National Park Service, Richmond Home Front office, November 2006.

Saxton, Alexander. *Bright Web in the Darkness.* Berkeley, CA: University of California Press, 1997.

Scherini, Rose and DiStasi, Lawrence with Adele Negro. *Una Storia Segreta.* Santa Cruz Public Library website.

Wollenberg, Charles. *Photographing the Second Gold Rush: Dorothea Lange and the Bay Area at War, 1941-1945.* Berkeley, CA: Heyday Books, 1995.

About the Author

Summer Brenner was raised in Georgia and migrated west, first to New Mexico and eventually to northern California where she has been a long-time resident. She has published nine books of poetry, fiction, and children's books, including *Ivy, Tale of a Homeless Girl in San Francisco*. In 2008, she received a grant from the Creative Work Fund to write *Richmond Tales: Lost Secrets of the Iron Triangle*.

Summer Brenner has worked in the Richmond community for fifteen years. In 2006, she began a collaboration with Community Works, and along with their director, Ruth Morgan, created "Where We're From," an inter-generational, cross-cultural oral history, poetry, and photography project for Richmond youth and their elders.

Summer Brenner is a board member of West County READS, a coalition of literacy advocates; and the Youth Transportation Coalition which works for free/reduced youth fare on public transit.

She is most proud of her two loving children, Felix Brenner and Joanna Bean.